# Sara's
## Turn of the Century

Kayla,
I hope you
enjoy the story!
Mary
2014

# Turn of the Century

Mary Prince

Published by Tate Publishing & Enterprises, LLC
127 E. Trade Center Terrace | Mustang, Oklahoma 73064 USA
1.888.361.9473 | www.tatepublishing.com

Tate Publishing is committed to excellence in the publishing industry. The company reflects the philosophy established by the founders, based on Psalm 68:11,
*"The Lord gave the word and great was the company of those who published it."*

Published in the United States of America

ISBN: 978-1-62902-164-5
1. Family & Relationships
2. Fiction / Christian / Romance
13.09.12

# CONTENTS

# Preface

Sara Watson was a bright, beautiful young woman, successful at about anything she touched. She lived in a small Southeastern Missouri town, where life had been good as she was growing up. Her family had moved to the country the summer she turned twelve. They lived in a modest ranch brick home with a large front porch and white columns set on two acres with beautiful trees and a bright green lawn, quite different than the yard she grew up in. She was raised in a Christian home and the family was of the Baptist faith. She attended church regularly. As a young teenager, she knew the importance of making the right choices; but like many she wavered here and there and had to ask forgiveness. She was a loving person and had a heart of gold, always caring about others in need, especially about children in poor countries that needed food, clothes, and shelter. She even insisted, when she was little, on writing to one as a pen pal and sending money to help, realizing early in life how fortunate and blessed she was.

She was all grown up now and it had been a pretty tough year. One day she jokingly said to her older brother,

Wayne, "Man, I could write a book about 1999!" She had no idea that the year she was about to face would have ***even more*** life altering hurdles; memorable . . . ***only*** if she ***survived*** them.

## Chapter 1

# 1999 Reflection

It was New Years Eve and what a year it had been! This New Years Eve celebration was not quite what she had anticipated. As she listened to "1999" by Prince, she thought back of one year ago and what led up to then . . .

There *were* some good qualities that had attracted her to her husband. Tommy intrigued her with his intelligence and artist flair. He was blonde, handsome, and a great dancer. She met him when she was attending a college in St. Louis, at a time when friends of a different lifestyle had entranced her. In high school she never had anything to do with people that were even around drugs; then ended up dating someone that took her to Raves where that atmosphere was all around her. Her style of clothes changed with these new friends, into the baggy sagging pants and graphic t-shirts. They dated for a while against the advice of family and old friends, including the high school boyfriend that she dated for three years and a college love who were both very good to her. Even she didn't know exactly "why" she seemed to be running away from her safe normal life.

After a few months of dating, they eloped! One weekend under the Arch, she and Tommy were married on a whim with promises of change and a better life than they were living. Sara got back to her normal self and left that short-lived life behind, but her husband couldn't seem to let go. His up bringing had been much different than hers. He was kind to her; that's one of the reasons she stayed. They seldom fought, except when he slipped back into the bad lifestyle! And even then it was not vicious word fights.

But after two years of anguish over his choices and nothing changing for the better, not even his work habits, Sara told him it was over; she was filing for a divorce. She asked him to move out of the house and made an appointment for January 5th to talk to a divorce attorney.

During this time, she got really sick with a stomach virus, or so she thought. When the nausea kept hanging on, a thought ran through her head one day. Could it be that she might be . . . oh no, she didn't even want to "think" the word! She left her home early that morning to go to the store and buy the dreaded test. Not that she would *dread* having a baby, just not *now*, not with *him*.

Sara went back home and as she patiently waited for the test to turn, she *prayed* for strength to handle the results. *(And STRENGTH she would need!)* Those few seconds seemed to take forever. "Oh man, could ***this*** be for ***real***?" she mumbled as she threw the *positive* test into the trash! Not totally convinced, she drove to the local Birthright office to confirm her results and that they did. The wait was over . . . she was **PREGNANT**! "What in the world? Why **NOW**, God?" she kept asking as left the office with her head spinning! There were no tears, just shock.

She drove directly home, taking one deep breath after the other, still in denial. Well, the first phone call had to be made...this is for *real*. "Mom?" she hesitated on the phone, and then said "I'm pregnant!" Her mom screamed, "*What*"? "Yep, you heard me!" Sara moaned. "Oh, honey are you sure?" her mom asked in disbelief. "Yes, a home test and Birthright were both positive," Sara replied. "But I thought you couldn't get pregnant" Mrs. Watson went on. "Are you going to tell Tommy right away?" she asked before Sara could even respond. *"I don't know, Mom!"* she said sounding frustrated. Then, with a sudden change of tone she squealed, "OMG! Can you believe I have a baby growing inside me?" "No, *actually,* I need time to even *process this!"* said Mrs. Watson. She would have been more excited for her daughter if their marriage had been more stable and Tommy more reliable. She knew he was not working at the time and when he did it was a part-time job at minimum wage. He was so smart but allowed his choices in life to influence what he made of himself. What kind of father was he going to be?

Sara couldn't resist, she hurried and drove out to see her mom *in person* that morning. Mrs. Watson was in the kitchen when she arrived. After a few seconds of silence when she walked in the back door, "It won't mess up college, Mom," Sara assured, "I might have to skip a semester next fall." Mrs. Watson was still processing the news with her face emotionless, "It'll be OK," she soothed, "I know you'll make the right decisions, honey." She gave her daughter a hug and apologized for her first response as they both were frozen in time and cried silent tears. Tears of joy mixed with fear of the complications this could bring to their life as a couple on the verge of dissolution of their marriage.

That New Year's Eve was a little strained. She made plans with Ashley, an old single girlfriend, to go out for a while. Ashley was an attractive redhead with a clear porcelain complexion and she had a fun personality. Sara wasn't dressed yet when she got there, so Ashley joined her in the bedroom as she tried on one outfit after another before she was finally content with one. She had a cute little body that looked good in anything she put on, but very hard to please, especially tonight.

"Sara, what are you gonna do?" asked Ashley. "Well I'm *having* this baby!" she snapped quickly. "No, that's not what I meant," said Ashley. "I know you better than that! I meant about the divorce." "I don't know," answered Sara. "Tommy will want to stay together even more now," she sighed. "You know," she said with a pause, "I thought I was infertile all this time, never used birth control and now here I am about to get a divorce when my body decides to work! Somehow, I just feel like this baby will be something special." "Do you think I could be a single mom?", she asked. "You?" smiled Ashley, "At the moment . . . I can't picture it!" shaking her head and laughing. Sara threw a pillow and hit her in the stomach.

"Let's get outta here!" she said as she smiled at her friend . . . as if to thank her for lightening the mood.

Sara and Ashley enjoyed the New Years celebration without any alcohol or cigarettes. They even joined her parents at the local Elks lodge. Since both girls were twenty-one, Mr. Watson offered to buy them a drink . . . but they gracefully declined. (Mom had not yet told him the news. She always wanted to protect him from stressful news and tried to pick just the right time to tell him.)

Everyone went on and on about how beautiful Sara & her friend were that evening and they gracefully showed their appreciation for the comments. The girls called it an early night, needless to say, no reason to party on into the night. They said their good-byes making it sound like they had someplace else to be, when that "someplace else" was *home*! Ashley stayed with her that night so Sara wouldn't bring in the New Year alone.

The next few days Sara was in a fog, but she went to work, as usual, like nothing had changed in her life. She was a good employee and successful at her position as an Inside Sales Rep. Her customers opened up to her on a regular basis, like they had known her for a long time. She was exceptional at making them feel at ease talking about their home, health, and families. She was genuine at caring for the families and their needs. Several years in a row she ranked in the *top three in the world* in her position with the company, she ranked third, second, and even *FIRST* a few times.

Sara went to the January 5th appointment. She answered all the attorney's questions honestly, even the one about the pregnancy but was surprised at what she heard. The attorney informed her that the law required a divorce *not be granted* until *after* she gave birth!

"No, No, No!" she sighed. "I'm afraid so, Sara," said her attorney. "You do realize that you can keep him at a distance until then, don't you?" "Yes, I understand but it just leaves a pain in the pit of my stomach. I hoped this would be quick and painless," Sara said, very disappointed.

At that point, she decided it was time to tell him about the baby. She called and said, "Tommy, we need to talk. Can you come to the house tonight after work?" "Sure," he said as he hung up the phone. He was just glad to be able to see her even though he knew the discussion would be about the divorce. He showed up about 8:00 and they sat down to talk. She told him of the appointment with the attorney, which he expected. But, what she told him next blew him away. They shared joy and tears even though their relationship was strained. "I'll do my best," he promised. "I know you'll be a great mom," he whispered, as he embraced her gently.

## Chapter 2

# Brother's Wedding

The month of January went by in a flash. Sara's brother, Wayne, was engaged and to be married in February. His fiancée, Jennifer, was a pretty girl with an amazing body and skin tone that didn't even need to tan. Sara was envious since she was so fair skinned.

Mr. Watson was the first to meet Jennifer; she worked part-time, between classes, at a convenience store drive-up window close by his work. He was impressed with her personality, as well as, her waistline and belly button visible from his car window (only in an appreciation of beauty kind of way!). She and Wayne met a while later and started dating, then engaged within a few months.

The family was busy with plans for the wedding, so that took some of the attention off of Sara, which she welcomed. Jennifer asked her to be a bridesmaid and she was honored. They were going with the Valentine's Day theme using red, white and black as their colors. Jennifer chose a red velour material and had the gowns custom made. They were absolutely stunning! Beautifully scooped neck in the front with a more daring scooped back; they had a fitted waist then flared to a flowing hemline, accenting each bridal attendant's unique figure.

A month and a half had past since the attorney told her she would have to *stay* married, and now she's getting ready to see her brother *get* married. "Thank God he really loves her," she thought, "Hopefully they will be happy and will last longer than her *two years*." Sara was never one to take the vows of marriage lightly. She believed that when you got married and made promises in God's presence that it was for *life* . . . for better or for worse.

She also believed that if she didn't get away from Tommy's lifestyle, it would definitely drag her down with him. That kind of life is no way to raise a baby! Her baby had to have the *best* and she would *die trying* to provide a good home. "Why am I thinking like this now?" she scolded herself, "This is *his* day and I'm happy for him!" She took a deep cleansing breath and joined the rest of the bridesmaids.

The florist forgot the corsage pins and there was no store close by, so Mrs. Watson went to work stitching on the flowers to each young man's lapel! She had brought a sewing kit in case the girl's dresses needed anything. This was a minor detail, but a fun memory for the bridal party.

The guests were all seated; the beautiful ladies in place and the handsome groomsmen were ready to escort each one down the isle. Jason, an old friend of theirs from high school, escorted Sara. That perked up her spirit, she always thought he was so handsome and that tux made him look like he just jumped out of the pages of GQ!

Jennifer's three-year old daughter, Elizabeth, was their flower girl. What a doll . . . she had a full head of dark brown hair and looked like an angel walking down the isle, spreading rose petals as she walked. Her dress was beautiful; it had come from their Aunt Carolyn's dress shop. Wayne and Sara's parents were pretty proud to have her as their first granddaughter!

She thought about Wayne's son, Austin, who was about the same age. He looked just like his dad in those early years. He lived with his mom, Stephanie, in another state so they didn't get to see each other as much as Wayne would like. But, he eventually came to terms with how their lives would be apart until he was old enough to come and stay a while. Wayne had loved Austin's mom but they were never married. She was married now and had another little boy. Wayne kept a good relationship going with her and tried to stay in touch for Austin's sake.

Back to the wedding at hand . . . Sara's mind was jumping all over the place. The music was nice, provided by Tim, a friend of Wayne's dad. He played the organ and did a really good job. The minister, Ernie, was a former Baptist preacher and good friend of his dad. The isle and archway were breathtaking, Jennifer had chosen red and white roses and it made a beautiful entrance (after several hours of hard labor the day before). Aunt Carolyn also dressed his mom for the occasion. As always, she had something picked out before his mom even got to her shop. She was a class act as she was escorted down the aisle in her sage green attire. So was Jennifer's mom, she had on a beautiful blue outfit.

The bride's dress was a gorgeous full-length beaded gown complete with a full train, and she carried a bouquet of red and white roses. She looked so pretty and happy as her dad walked her down the isle! Wayne was all jittery and heart pounding. Sara knew him well enough to just look at him and tell. She gave him a quick reassuring smile when he looked her way. They were going to be fine . . . she just knew it.

After the ceremony, they took some of the wedding pictures outside the lodge by the lake. It started to snow lightly before they were done. The banquet hall had full windows facing the lake, so their guests were able to watch from inside and even let out a few "ahs" when it started to snow. It was a beautiful setting as the snow came down!

While they were outside, the decorating crew transformed the banquet hall from "chapel" to "reception". The runner and all chairs had to be taken down and stored. The tables had nice, soft dining chairs and were decorated with white tablecloths and red roses in a white vase as centerpieces. Each vase had a black ribbon tied around it. It was a classy look.

Wayne looked especially handsome in his tuxedo. Sara was proud of him. He had always liked to sing and had a *pretty darn good* voice! He and his new bride sang the Shania Twain & Brian White's song "From This Moment On", looking into each other's eyes with their faces almost touching at times. They really got into it leaving almost everyone speechless or tearing up, especially the ladies.

When it was time to cut the cake, there was a slight mishap. The night before, Jennifer's Mom and Mrs. Watson, had worked *into the nigh*t making their beautiful wedding cake. It was four-layers with pretty good roses and other decorations for two amateurs. It had transported very well, but by the time they were ready to take pictures it was *leaning* a little too much! The two came to the rescue to do some emergency work and save the cake. All was good. As the bride and groom shared their first piece, both ended up with a little icing on their faces. They entertained the guests as they proceeded to lick each other's face! Jennifer and Wayne made a fun couple.

Sara had started to show a little by now; her tiny frame didn't take much. She looked amazing in the red velour gown, but changed into something looser for the rest of the evening. Not many people knew about the pregnancy, only close friends and immediate family. Most everyone knew she was leaving Tommy and agreed that it was the right move. She was glad that she wasn't the topic of conversation that day. She enjoyed the reception and danced a few times but tired easily. Seeing family members from out of town was nice. Her dad was the baby of the family and so was she, therefore, cousins were older than her and married . . . most with children. And they were all crazy about Sara. She ate it up of course.

For a three-year old, Elizabeth had some endurance. She had a great time and danced almost every dance with either a grown-up or several other kids and lasted longer than some adults! She finally gave out and fell asleep on

Grandpa's jacket behind the head table after they saw the bride and groom off. She was already calling Wayne "Dad". He was glad to have her as a daughter; she was so precious! Her dad lived in another state and wasn't around at all. Mom and Dad had never married . . . very similar to Wayne's situation with Austin. But now she had a *family.* Her new grandparents gladly volunteered to keep her for the weekend while they enjoyed their honeymoon.

# Chapter 3

# The News

Sara had planned on finishing the semester at the local university while still working. That schedule had been working fine and she thought the walking back and forth to classes would be good exercise for her. Classes were going well, she was able to study enough and still work full-time. She didn't expect the pregnancy to hold her back. It was just like Sara to think that way; she had been a hard worker since she was 14 years old. She had a stubborn streak like her daddy, which made them both tough achievers.

Tommy had come back into the picture and was trying to do better. She didn't want to keep him totally annihilated. He was great company for her on his good days and would give her foot rubs after a long day of school and work.

Then one night of *panic* made her take a few steps back and changed her life dramatically! They were sleeping when Sara awoke with a strong urge to go to the bathroom. As she walked, she felt moisture and when she sat down she let out a horrific scream, "Tommy! Oh my God, ***HURRY***!" She was bleeding pretty badly. He tried to calm her as he got her coat, "You're going to the hospital, honey. This doesn't look good." "Call my mom, she'll meet us there," she said trying to calm herself. Tommy called after he got her in the car. He started explaining and she interrupted him and said, "Just get her to the ER, I'll be right there!"

The hospital was only a few blocks from where they lived so it only took minutes. Tommy parked the car outside the emergency room doors and helped her inside. "Help me," he cried out, "My wife's pregnant and she's bleeding!" A nurse came out of the triage and brought her a wheelchair. She instructed Tommy to sign her in while she checked her vitals. Moments later, she was taken to an exam room and got undressed from the waist down. The nurse was kind and concerned for her baby; she placed a pad beneath her for the bleeding.

The ER doctor examined her only briefly before ordering an ultrasound. Their awkward waiting period started at that point, the normal ER routine. "What do you say at a time like this, except pray?" Mrs. Watson stated to break the silence. Sara just looked at Tommy with a worried glare. She had already started to enjoy the thought of a baby growing in her belly and knew it was a miracle that she even conceived at all.

Finally, they came to get her for the ultrasound. During the examination they saw the baby moving and heard its little heart beating! All three of their faces were in *awe*; they couldn't help but cry, especially her mom. She cried as she put her hands to her chest, "There's just something overwhelming about seeing your *grandbaby* inside your *daughter* that's indescribable!" Sara had tears rolling down her cheeks as she pointed to the screen and softly said, "*That'*s my baby!" She didn't want the ultrasound to end; she couldn't take her eyes off the screen for more than a second.

When back in her room, the doctor came in with *horrible news*. He said, "I'm so sorry, but you're losing this baby. You have a six-inch uterine bleed and there is *no way the baby can survive that*." Sara was frozen in grief for several seconds then started defiantly sobbing . . . "NO, NO, I just saw my baby and it's just *fine*!" The doctor again expressed his sympathy and told her to follow up with her regular doctor within a few days. He said a nurse would be in with information on dealing with a miscarriage.

Her mom tried consoling them without much success, she was heartbroken too. The tears just kept on falling. It was a long, long night. They took Sara back home after the bleeding subsided and helped her get into bed. She said through her tears, "After all this time, why would God give me a baby *now* and then take it away from me?" Her mom consoled, "Honey, sometimes our bodies just don't cooperate with the *miracle of conception.*" She went on home, but it was so very hard to leave her daughter that night. "You know that all you have to do is call and I'll be right here", she said as she left the room, "I love you, honey." "Love you too, Mom," Sara replied.

The external bleeding had stopped completely by the time she saw her family doctor a few days later. Dr. Griffith had delivered lots of babies over the years so they trusted him completely. Sara told him what the emergency doctor had said. He was angry that the doctor came to that conclusion so quickly. Another ultrasound was ordered before he made too many comments. It was scheduled for the next morning.

The second ultrasound confirmed the uterine bleed . . . and it was at least 6 inches in length. But, at the same time, the baby still seemed to be doing fine . . . heartbeat, movement, development, etc., all normal! On one view, they saw it was a **BOY**! On another view his little hand seemed to be waving to them, as if to say, "***Hey guys . . . I'm OK***!"

After that Sara's heart was filled with hope even as the doctor continued, on her next appointment, to tell her of the uterine condition. Dr. Griffith told her something that eased the pain ever so slightly. He said, "Sara, if you really want to save this baby, you will stay off your feet, I mean totally . . . *complete bed rest* except for bathroom and shower. Then your baby may have a chance to survive . . . God willing." She thanked him and left the office clinging to the ultrasound picture of her baby, waving his little hand!

She was now three months into the pregnancy and determined to do *everything* she could to save this baby! She left Tommy for good to reduce the stress in her life. As it turned out, his *best* was just not good enough for Sara. He dropped out of the picture without much resistance.

She contacted her landlord and told him she would have to move out before the lease was up. With it being a medical reason, he was very nice about releasing her. Sara felt awful that she couldn't be there during the move and couldn't lift a finger to help with her own stuff. Her mom did all the packing up; later friends and family came over to carry everything out. Most everything went into storage except her *three cats and two dogs,* one of which was a *hyper Dalmatian* named Max! Her parents "graciously" accepted the pets, even though they already had Brandy, a Cocker Spaniel; Maggie, a Black Lab; and two indoor cats, Bootie and Buster. They felt like their house was becoming a kennel! Her black dog was a mixed breed and very sweet, the daughter of Maggie, but she got hit and killed in the road not long after that. Max on the other hand, was a crazy dog. They found him a home with a single older lady with a fenced in yard for him to run to his heart's content. She had no other pets and needed his company.

On her next doctor visit, he told her that she could not be around cat litter at all. He highly suggested no cats because being around cat litter could add to the chance of miscarriage. It broke their hearts but they found homes for all five cats. Sara's mom was really close to Buster and missed him a lot. He was a calm cat with beautiful long black hair with a little white under his chin and down his neck. He used to wake her in the morning with a soft brush of his paw on her cheek. Her dad had always been a cat lover and even he said they all have to go; he wouldn't chance anything hurting his grandson!

Sara had to drop out of college, of course, and promised herself to finish someday. She also asked for a leave from her job. Her parents made her comfortable in her old room. They moved out the twin bed and brought in a full size with a brand new mattress set. Mom served her three complete meals everyday and made sure she always had something to drink. She brought her books to read including her bible. One of her favorite books was "Chicken Soup for Mothers". She loved reading stories of other mothers and the struggles they went through. Mom would come in and catch her crying over someone else's pain, and realizing that her own situation was not as grim at the moment. There were stories of extended illnesses, severe handicaps, and heart wrenching grief from the loss of a child. The stories helped her count her blessings.

She prayed one night, "God, please don't give up on me . . . I can be the person you want me to be and I can be a good mom. Please bless my baby's life and let him be born healthy. Your will be done, in Jesus name, Amen." She continued to pray everyday and sometimes several times a day. God has a way of pulling you close to him again and He had done that for Sara! She had her faith back; she saw the world in a new light and felt God's grace surrounding her. The family asked for prayers from family, friends, co-workers, and everyone at church and even called on prayer partners from all over the country to pray for a miracle. Her maternal grandmother was the song leader at her church in Mississippi. She started prayer chains all across the state.

As Sara improved emotionally, she felt able to handle some work from home. She talked her employer into letting her work from her bed. She had worked for the company several years and she was a very productive employee. They were glad to accommodate her. They brought her files and set up at her bedside. She used the phone to continue making money, as she was bedridden. It was very fortunate that *talking on the phone* was the main part of her job.

Everyone that knew Sara admired her strength, hope, determination, and tenacity. She ate only healthy foods and never mentioned wanting a cigarette, knowing the effects on the baby. She had started smoking as a teenager, one of those rebellious things. She had already been trying to quit when she found out about the baby, so that news sealed the deal on that habit. With that small thin frame, the pregnancy weight really changed her body. She took it in stride and enjoyed watching her body grow as the baby, now called Jacob, grew and matured insider her. She was completely obedient to the rules of staying in bed. The doctor ordered frequent ultrasounds to keep an eye on the size of the uterine bleed and monitor Jacob's development. She loved feeling him move around. All the while, praying that God would bless her child and help him survive.

## Chapter 4

# Strength of Faith

In April that year, Sara's grandfather (mom's dad), died of a ten-year battle with emphysema. They lived in Mississippi so she was not able to attend the funeral. Her mom went with her sister, Aunt Sue, leaving the rest of the family to take care of her and serve the necessary meals in bed.

Sara's mother was from a family of twelve kids with Aunt Sue the oldest and her mom second. They had lost Peggy, next sister in line, from pneumonia at the age of two, so eleven were left.

She really enjoyed traveling with her sister. They would always get into a laughing frenzy at least once on each trip! This trip was not a happy one but she still loved her company; they could talk the whole five hours, non-stop.

The day of the funeral the whole family had gathered at their parents' house. Aunt Sue and a few others got ready and went on to the funeral home with their mom. Sara's mom stayed behind and would come with the rest of the family. What she had to handle the remainder of the day was not your *typical funeral.*

Her sister, Ima, suddenly started crying with a really bad headache. Everyone thought she was just upset about her dad and that her blood pressure was probably up. They all tried to console her, getting cold cloths and a bag to breathe into, hoping to settle her down. When she was standing beside Ima hugging her shoulder, she threw up and was so apologetic as she cried in severe pain! Nobody cared about the mess . . . they just wanted to help her. At that point, everyone was getting scared that it was more than just being upset, so they called 911. As soon as the paramedics got there, she passed out and had to be lifted onto the gurney. Some of the family immediately followed the ambulance, while some went on to the funeral and reported to their mom what had happened. She, too, thought her daughter was upset and would be fine.

Meanwhile at the hospital, after what seemed like an extremely long wait; the doctor came out and said she had a massive cerebral hemorrhage and it didn't look good. He continued to say that they were rushing her by helicopter to Memphis. While the family was trying to deal with what he just said . . . a nurse reported she had gotten worse and the transport to Memphis had been cancelled.

Sara's mom had to step away and pull herself together. She just realized that she had to be the one to take the news to her *mother.* She called home and told the family the tragic news. Mrs. Watson was going to need a few more days with her mom. They assured that Sara was doing okay and being taken care of. They expressed their concern for her family with prayers and deep heartfelt sympathy.

She got to the funeral just as the service was starting and purposely sat a couple rows back from her mom. She nodded and barely put up a hand when her mom looked at her. How could she tell her that she is *loosing her daughter* today? She prayed silently, “Oh my Lord and Savior, please give this dear woman the strength to handle what she’s about to face!” The service seemed to go on forever and people were whispering about Ima. She would just give them a worried look and shake her head no. When it finally ended, she went to Sue first; she needed her strength as they went to their mom together. She hugged her then took both her hands and held them tight as she said through tears, “Mom . . . she’s had a *massive brain hemorrhage* and the doctors don’t expect her make it.” Her mom said, “Oh, NO”, and they had to catch her as she went weak. After about a minute, when she caught her breath, she said, “We’ll cut the cemetery service short so I can get to her, Daddy will understand.”

The family sat for hours that night waiting and taking turns to go in to see Ima. She was hooked up to all kinds of equipment and was never responsive. They seemed to be just giving all the family time to get there and giving them time to prepare for the news of her death, which was around midnight. She went to heaven leaving her mom, ten siblings, husband, daughter, son, and two grandbabies. Everyone would remember this jolly, big-hearted woman with tender memories. Everybody loved her.

It was horrible dealing with both deaths, but their mother was a pillar of strength through the planning and during the funerals. She said Christ was holding her up!

What an example of faith for everyone! Sara's mom and Aunt Sue waited until the day after to head home. It was a tearful trip home, but they felt their mom would be all right; she was a tough lady. She had to be tough to raise a family that size.

It was nice getting back home to Sara; her mom didn't like being away from her that long. She was alone most of the day while she was gone because everyone else was working. They hugged and cried as Sara whispered, "I'm so sorry, Mom".

## Chapter 5

# Preparing for Baby

After three long months, the doctor released Sara from bed rest. She still had to take it easy, but everything seemed to be doing fine. There were concerns that Jacob could come prematurely, so she followed the doctor's orders and started preparing for her baby. The whole family pitched in to help; every free minute seemed to be dedicated to this little guy. They were very generous with their time and energy.

Her bedroom was turned into a nursery with blue and white striped wallpaper on two walls, one wall white, and wallpaper with clouds and blue sky on the wall by the baby bed. A Precious Moments border, with clouds and blue sky, was put up around the ceiling. The bedspread was a matching shade of blue. A changing table was placed close to Sara's bed to finish off the nursery.

Tommy ended up being very immature, not handling things very well, and continued making his bad choices. Therefore, there were emotional ups and downs to deal with. Sara didn't want to keep him out of Jacob's life, but his actions made her think along those terms.

During this time, Wayne & Jennifer were expecting too. Their baby was due in December. Elizabeth would be four on December 7th, so they were expecting a busy December. It had already been a very busy 1999 for the family.

Sara's friend, Kari, gave her an elaborate baby shower with a white tent, balloons, and the whole works. It was summer and the weather was perfect. She wore a loose sleeveless blue dress and sandals with her hair down and was smiling all day! Aunts and cousins from out of town came. Several friends from work, school, and church showed up; it was a great turnout. She appreciated the necessary items and the pretty things received. Mom made her a big t-shirt that said "Jacob on Board" with a stork and baby artwork by her dad. It was one of those souvenir things you keep forever.

To everyone's surprise, her pregnancy lasted full term and Jacob seemed to be doing pretty good in there. The doctor didn't want to take any chances with the drama that can be associated with going into labor. He mentioned making plans to go in the next week. She was admitted to the hospital on August 18th to induce labor. (Mrs. Watson actually chose the date so his birthday could be 8-19-99.) Sara was thankful to make it this long, so she was all for it. She was a beautiful pregnant lady with glowing skin. She ended up with 60 additional pounds on that small frame!

She was a real trooper all through labor, so positive and happy that she was about to be able to hold him in her arms. Kari sat through hours of labor with her then decided to go out at 11:00 that night to buy a baby name book. Sara had not yet come up with a middle name, so they had something to pass the time!

They had lots of laughs that night; her mom, brother, and best friend entertained her. Her dad came by for a while, but didn't stay for the duration. Hospitals were not his thing; especially seeing his little girl in pain!

She managed to catch a few winks between contractions, but by morning she was worn out. After a final check for dilation, the nurse announced that she was calling Dr. Griffith. The baby was ready! Everything went real smooth, no complications so far and time seemed to fly at that point.

After all these months of fear, hope, and prayer . . . Jacob Carson was born . . . a healthy 8 lb. 10 oz. baby boy. He was, without a doubt, Sara's little miracle! "Thank you, God" she whispered, as she kissed his precious little head. Tears ran down her face as she smiled from ear to ear. She could finally hold him in her arms and he was *absolutely perfect!* Grandma and Grandpa were overwhelmed . . . this was the first grandchild they experienced being born. What a miracle of life!

Those few months had strengthened Sara's faith in God and His Son, Jesus Christ. He *did* answer prayers! "This little guy should surely have a blessed life", she said after a few minutes of holding him, "He was certainly *meant to be.*" There was a great amount of rejoicing of friends, family, and all those praying for this young lady and her baby boy.

Tommy came by the hospital and a picture was taken of him admiring his son. You could tell that he loved him, but was reserved. He was happy for him & Sara, but not one to be involved in Jacob's life.

Wayne and Jennifer were anxious to come in and see their nephew. Wayne just couldn't wait for her to get in a room . . . he was a new uncle. "He's awesome, Sara!" he said, as he bent down and hugged her with Jacob in her arms. "I know," she said, "Can you believe it?" She was pumped with adrenalin; her heart was pounding in her chest.

The nursing came natural for her and he latched right on like he had been practicing. "How do they know how to do that?" she asked mom. "It's a God given, natural instinct for survival" she answered. "WOW!" said Sara.

Everything went well for both mom and baby boy so she was able to go home the next day. Preparing to leave the security of the hospital made her a little nervous. She had a shower and shampooed her hair. Put on a slight amount of make-up and pulled her hair back in a headband, then dressed in a navy blue outfit of loose pants and sleeveless top. Sara took her time and got him dressed in a cute white outfit with blue trim. She brushed his hair, parted on the left side and combed it over. She then wrapped him in a soft blue blanket to keep him snug and warm. As they were wheeled out to the car, she also carried a bouquet of lilies in her lap that her dad had brought her. Of course, Mom had a camera and stopped them for a picture before they got in the car. Jacob looked so tiny as he was being buckled in the rear-facing car seat for the first time.

When she brought Jacob home Sara was surprised with a big sign with blue balloons by the driveway; it was a big baby in a diaper saying: "It's a BOY!" She knew Dad had to be the one to put it up because Mom was the one driving her home. He was good about stuff like that, but he was gone golfing when they got there. Their home was out in the country but on a main highway, so it was the feeling of "the country" with easy access. The multiple flower gardens were in full bloom and beautiful to come home to.

The nursery area was broken in real quick; Jacob needed changing right away. She was glad she had received a *Diaper Genie* for a shower gift since it was a #2 diaper! And wipes, from the *warmer*, were really nice and soothing for his bare bottom. "How things change from one generation to another," said Mrs. Watson...shaking her head as she was leaving the room. "Where you goin' Mom?" asked Sara. "You'll get the hang of it...*practice* makes perfect." She smiled as she went down the hallway.

One of Sara's favorite things about being a new mom was the baby nursing. She was glad to be able to nurse for the nutrients *and* the *emotional connection*. She would not take her eyes off him at first; she watched every little move he'd make the whole time he nursed. And he was an *eater*, nothing wrong with his appetite! She was thankful that she made plenty of milk. She knew that some moms don't and it's a huge letdown for those who had their heart set on nursing.

Grandma & Grandpa were glad to have them living there. They got to spoil him for her and Grandpa tried to fill in as his father figure. He was shocked at how he was affected by this bundle of joy; he *fell in love* with Jacob! He wasn't a good sleeper at night, so in the mornings Grandpa would take him and let Sara get in a little more sleep. Every morning he would lay him on the foot of their bed and stand over him just soaking him up. He couldn't believe how beautiful and perfect he was, not obviously affected by the problems in her womb. He would give Jacob a full body massage and you could tell, even as an infant, that he loved it as much as Grandpa loved giving it.

As he grew to be a few months old . . . out came the laughter. They would wake up everybody else in the house with their laughs. He was so precious! Dozens of pictures were taken at every little change he went through. It was a wonderful and memorable time for them all. Jacob was their little miracle!

Because of Tommy's choice not to change his life, she went ahead with the divorce in the fall. It was uncontested and final in October, along with signing off on his parental rights.

Sara was upset that the choice she had made in marrying Tommy had been a mistake, except for the fact that the union made Jacob. Wayne had left a long note for her when he came by one night when she was at work, it read as follows:

"Sara,

People come into our life for a *reason*, a *season,* or a *lifetime*. When you realize which one it is, you'll know what to do for that person. When someone is in your life for a "reason", it is usually to meet a need you've expressed. They have come to assist you through a difficulty, to provide you with guidance or support, to aid you physically, emotionally, and/or spiritually. They may seem like a "Godsend" at the time and they may be. They are there for the reason you need them to be. Then, without any wrongdoing on your part or at an awkward time, this person will say or do something to bring the relationship to an end. Sometimes they die! Sometimes they walk away. Sometimes they act out and force you to take a stand. What we have to realize is that our need has been met, our desire fulfilled, their work is done. The prayer you've sent up has been answered and now it's time to move on! Some people come into our life as a "season" because your turn has come to share, grow, and bloom. They bring you an experience of peace or may make you laugh. They may teach you something you've never done, or show you something you've never seen. They usually give you an unbelievable amount of joy. Believe it, it is for real! But it's like leaves on a tree; it's only for a season!

Good "lifetime" relationships teach you lifetime lessons, things you must build upon in order to have a solid emotional foundation. You have to accept the lesson, love the person, and put what you've learned to use in all your other relationships and areas of your life. It is said that you never know what you have until it's gone . . . well you never know what you've been missing until it arrives! Relationships are important . . . all types. Always remember that love is blind but friendship is clairvoyant!

Live your life to the fullest, Sara! You only have one life, so why not make the best of it? Don't waste your time waiting on the past to make sense . . . it's over! You have total control of your future. You're destined to be special and remember you're someone that matters. Don't let anyone treat you less! Look in the mirror and say "I am ***Sara Watson*** and the ***mother*** of an ***amazing little boy***! I can DO this "***through Christ who strengthens me***" with or without a significant other!

I love you, Sis!"

"Wow," she said out loud. With that, Sara was relieved and glad that she had kept her maiden name. "That was amazing, didn't know my brother had it in him!" she said, handing it to her mom, "You gotta read this!"

# Chapter 6

# Another Baby?

After Thanksgiving they all knew Jennifer was due anytime. Sara and Mrs. Watson gave her a baby shower a few weeks before. She got a blue hand crocheted afghan from Wayne's best friend's mom, and lots of the basic necessities along with really cute clothes. Elizabeth had a blast getting stuff ready for her new brother. She knew that she and the baby would be sharing a room for a while, but that was fine with her because she anticipated getting a *live* baby doll!

Jennifer had an uneventful pregnancy, unlike Sara. She ate just about anything she wanted but still didn't gain too much weight. She was a pretty pregnant lady. December 1st rolled around and this was the day. The family will never forget Edward's entry into this world!

When she went to the hospital that day, she asked both grandmas to give them space and watch from a distance until they were told to come in. This was at the time when birthing rooms were larger to accommodate family and close friends, as long as they were *welcomed*.

Her labor was long and very painful! Since this was her second time around, that could be why she didn't want people in the room. The doctor tried the epidural several times, but it was not effective. She let anyone within distance hear her frustrated remarks! Wayne tried to help, but it was like one of those television shows of the mom biting the dad's head off. It was Wayne's first birth experience and it was a memorable one.

Both grandmas and her sister were watching and listening from an adjoining room. They tried to be quiet, but the reactions to Jennifer's remarks would make them gasp at the least. They all felt for her and prayed that it would soon be over. After a while, they got a little delirious. Wayne's mom tried to lean over and see a little better, she fell over making a loud noise and setting off a giggling frenzy! They quickly tried to regain their composure to keep from getting kicked out completely.

After many hours of labor, Edward was finally ready to enter his new world, or *maybe not.* After coming through the birth canal, he didn't want to take that first breath . . . it seemed so very long as they all silently waited. Seconds seemed like minutes as the nurses worked with his little body to no avail. Every fruitless effort stunned the surrounding family members. Tears streamed down Wayne's face as his heart was about to explode. Jennifer couldn't breathe. The whole room was silently praying for his life. This moment was being video taped; it seemed like a slow motion movie. The little guy was definitely center stage when he finally sucked in a breath and let out a *very welcomed cry!* Edward checked out perfectly healthy after that dramatic entrance. He was so beautiful, looking like his dad and sister, with his mom's gorgeous skin color. Jennifer was exhausted, Wayne was elated, and Elizabeth was obviously very proud of her little brother. They all were thanking God for that first breath.

He was an awesome baby boy! He slept thru the night from the beginning, opposite of his cousin, Jacob. Sara loved him, but was jealous of the restful sleep Jennifer was able to get, as she wondered how a person could even function on as little as she had the last four months.

The family loved getting together and comparing the two boys and their differences; even their personalities were totally different as young as they both were. They looked forward to watching them grow up together. Elizabeth was in heaven playing the "mother hen" to both the boys. Being so young, it was amazing how great she was with the babies. She had celebrated her fourth birthday just six-days after her brother was born.

Decorating for Christmas meant even more that year; the family had a lot to be thankful for as they prepared to celebrate the Birth of Jesus. Mrs. Watson put herself in Mary's place for a few moments as she put out the manger scene and wondered how she must have felt when she was preparing to give birth to the Holy Child.

The house was decorated with lights outside along the front of the house and along the roof of a lawn building out back. Wayne helped his parents with the lights as always. The tree was centered in the living room picture window and looked beautiful from the road. The wall adjacent from the tree had lighted greenery, which was also visible. Their family room had a vaulted ceiling with a brick fireplace at the end of the long room; the whole wall around the fireplace was bricked. Wayne and Mr. Watson put lighted garland along the ceiling of that wall and a lighted manger scene on the mantle. Red candles in brass candleholders were placed on each side and stockings were hung for the kids and grandkids.

This was always Mrs. Watson's favorite time of year, but this year seemed truly blessed with their two new babies. She reflected on the year of Sara's bed rest and Jacob's miraculous survival, losing her dad and sister, and Edward's God-given first breath. *Blessings and heartaches* was how that year would be remembered.

# Chapter 7

# Another Hurdle

What a year! But wait . . . December was not over yet and neither were the shocks or heartaches!

While on a shopping trip with her mom and baby Jacob, Sara mentioned some zinging pain in the side of her head. It was very localized and like nothing either one of them had experienced before. Mrs. Watson immediately called up the family doctor, Dr. Griffith, who was very conscientious, and reported her daughter's pain. After what happened to her sister earlier this year, she wasn't taking any chances!

He promptly ordered a CT scan of her head the next day. Sara waited calmly as she and her mom played with Jacob. They were waiting to hear that the films were fine and they could go home, expecting to wait a few days to hear the results. After a while longer, the radiologist came out himself. (This gave her a sick feeling in her stomach . . . NEVER had she heard of a doctor coming out to speak with the patient after a CT.) He showed them the films that indicated a problem with *blood vessels in her brain*! Sara had an AVM *(Arterio-Venous Malformation)* and was being referred to Barnes Hospital in St. Louis for further evaluation. They were told how fortunate she was to find this problem; most people don't even get to hear they have one before a hemorrhage happens. They left with the films, but somehow they didn't feel very fortunate, more like stunned. They didn't talk all the way home, just played and pacified Jacob.

Dr. Griffith was called the next morning. Mrs. Watson started the conversation with, "Thank you for ordering the scan so quickly. Now what?" He replied, "The neuro team at Barnes will give her a thorough evaluation and recommend the appropriate treatment." He said, "It's a miracle that you still have her. We could have lost her when Jacob was born." "Oh, my goodness," she said almost breathless. "Women have died during the pushing stage of childbirth with this condition, most not having a clue anything was wrong," he continued. "I guess God sent us two miracles that day . . . thank you again, Dr. Griffith," she said with tears welling up as she hung up the phone. It was her first time to cry since the news yesterday. He just made the severity of her daughter's condition really sink in. Chills went down her spine as she wondered what they were up against.

She went into the bedroom where Sara was dressing Jacob. She looked up smiling and saw her mother's tears. "What?" "What did he say?" she asked back to back. "He confirmed what the doctor said yesterday," she whispered. "But we know yours is there and we'll get it fixed," her mom continued, as she put her arm around her daughter and admired her little miracle child. She silently asked God for one more miracle.

Barnes Hospital got her in with a neurosurgeon right away. He did a thorough exam and asked lots of questions. He shared the films with Sara and her mom and showed them the AVM. This malformation was a mass of tangled arteries and veins that wasn't allowing the blood to flow properly in her brain. He was amazed that she had no symptoms until now. He looked at Jacob and nodded, "What a miracle we have here!"

Sara asked, "So what do we do now? Can you cut it out?" "It's not that simple, Miss Sara," he said (almost like he was apologizing that he couldn't just *fix* it). "You'll need further tests with a team of specialists for the best outcome," he continued. "We'll get the appointments set up; the first step will be a neuro-angiogram." "What's that?" asked Sara. "Well, it's where they put a tiny camera/catheter in your thigh artery and feed it carefully all the way up to your brain," he explained. "It's a non-invasive way to show what we're dealing with." "I'll answer more questions as soon as we know more. Feel free to call anytime, but if you experience extreme pain in your head, get to the nearest ER and have them call *me,*" he concluded. "You all go home and have a Merry Christmas. Enjoy this little guy."

They left with heavy hearts, too upset by Sara's condition to discuss it much on the way home. Tears were fought back as much as possible, but the lump in both their throats was obvious. They were glad Jacob was there to help ease the tension, this *little guy* had no idea what a *blessing* he really was!

When Mr. Watson and Wayne got home from work that evening, they all sat down for a family conference. This was not something they wanted to repeat several times at the moment. They sat the kids in the floor and gathered around the kitchen table. Mrs. Watson and Sara tried to remember everything the neuro-surgeon had said at the appointment to share with the family. Now the tears were not held back, but they tried to hold it together enough to get through all the information shared about the condition in her brain. Everyone did their best to say something comforting and hopeful for Sara's sake. They knew she was in God's hands, and had to believe that she was going to survive.

# Chapter 8

# Christmas Romance

The family tried to go ahead with plans for Christmas while waiting for the next appointment. They enjoyed the kids' different ages. . . Elizabeth now four, Jacob four months, and Edward a couple weeks. They loved the decorations and lights on the tree. Elizabeth liked driving around after dark looking at all the Christmas lights. And it was always eventful when they tried to go Christmas shopping with the kids.

While at an office Christmas party, Sara ran into Adam Taylor, an old friend from high school. He had grown up and filled out . . . tall and very *handsome*! He had dark brown hair (almost black) and it was a little wavy. His face had matured in a nice way with a *gorgeous* smile. His jeans and blue sweater complimented his physique.

Sara was at her best that night, too. Her bust was fuller from nursing; she had on an ivory sweater and pants to match, high-heel brown boots, with her long flowing blonde hair and green eyes. She was a knock out!

They hit it off and started talking about "days gone by". She felt surges through her body just being near him! This was going to cause trouble . . . he was dating Alyssa, a friend from work. As the night progressed they kept being drawn to each other from across the room. They ended up leaving the party together when he offered her a ride home. She had ridden there with a co-worker so that was fine with her. The problem was he had planned on going back to the party to take his date home, too. Well, that didn't happen . . . they talked and touched lightly here and there . . . then the KISS happened and things progressed pretty quickly. The touch of his hand and his warm kiss ignited something in her that she thought was gone for forever.

He swept her off her feet and the kisses soon became passionate! It was hard to say goodnight...they wanted the night to never end. But it did and reality hit when he remembered that he had left Alyssa alone at the party. That was going to take some explaining!

Sara had not gone out looking for romance. She had enough going one in her life. "What in the world was I thinking," she said to herself the next day. It was going to be really awkward at work; even though she didn't think Adam and Alyssa were that serious she would never intentionally pursue a friend's guy. It just happened! As she relived the night, it was *worth* it! Maybe Alyssa would eventually understand.

She just had to talk to her mom after breakfast. She went into the bathroom and sat on the edge of the tub while Mrs. Watson was washing her face. "Mom, you wouldn't believe last night." "Did you have a good time at the party?" she asked. "Uh . . . Yeah! And AFTER the party!

Remember Adam Taylor from high school?" "I think so, was he tall and skinny?" asked her mom. "Yeah, but he has filled out and very handsome" swooned Sara.

Their first actual date was that next week. He met her in town and stood at his truck with a rose behind his back. He must have done all the right things because she said to her mom the next day, "I think he's the *one* to spend the rest of my life with. Last night was *wonderful*!" Her mom just smiled at her daughter's swooning and shook her head. "Don't rush into anything, honey," she warned.

Adam and Sara saw each other almost every day the rest of the month of December. He was between jobs and waiting on a great job with a union; so he had plenty of daytime hours to spend with her and Jacob. She told him about the problem in her head but even that didn't scare him off.

It was a wonderful, yet strained, Christmas for the whole family that year. They rejoiced in the children, while silently worrying about Sara. The family attended the Christmas Eve Candlelight Service at church; it was a good reminder that Jesus is the "reason for the season". Of course, the excitement of Santa the next morning had the kids entertained. Mr. & Mrs. Watson tried hard to keep the atmosphere as cheerful as possible, while praying the Lord would continue to bless their children and grandchildren.

Christmas dinner was interesting with the babies. Aunt Sue and Uncle Lee had joined them for dinner. They never had children, so it was especially different for them even though they seemed to have a good time.

They were a pretty cool couple and always went with the flow.

The week after Christmas was just "going through the motions" for the family with kids and work. Even with the new romance, the new millennium had *lost its luster*. The fears of a system meltdown, which was in the news all year long, had been *overshadowed*.

Grandma and Grandpa offered to stay home and keep all three kids that New Year's Eve. They knew the young parents needed a night out to socialize and unwind. Bringing in the "turn of the century" didn't come along with the anticipated partying for this family though; *life had gotten in the way*.

## Chapter 9

# Back to 2000

Back from her thoughts . . . Sara took a deep breath, exhaled, and with a smile suggested a toast. "Oh well, bring on the year 2000!" Everyone wondered *where* in the past year she just *went*, but nobody asked . . . they just joined her toast. Wayne said, "Hell yeah!" Adam added, "We can handle it!" Jennifer joined in with, "You go girl!", as they tapped their glasses to the New Year.

They had joined other friends at a local club; the live band was good and a lot of people were on the dance floor most of the night. Adam, admiring his date, ran his fingers through a strand of her soft hair and breathed in her scent. Sara loved dancing; and being in Adam's arms felt so good. When he placed his hand on the small of her back she just melted. Even with her high-heels, he was so much taller that her head lay on his chest. She felt intoxicated even though there was no alcohol for her that night. (Breast feeding Jacob was much more important to her.)

Jen was only four weeks out from childbirth; so she didn't *get down* to the music like she normally did. Wayne slow danced with her and joined her with a few faster tunes, too. That kind of dancing wasn't his first love; but he wanted to make her happy. She always loved dancing and was really good at it. His favorite was country line dancing. He and Sara used to teach other teenagers steps at the park with their car stereos blasting country music.

The count down to the New Year "2000" was announced! "Ten, nine, eight, seven, six, five, four, three, two, one . . . HAPPY NEW YEAR!!! Cheers exploded in the room along with party pop streamers. Wayne and Adam looked at their women with admiration as they embraced and kissed in the New Year. Sara had never had a dress-up New Year's Eve celebration like this before; her heart was racing! The band played the traditional "Auld Lang Syne" music and everyone joined in the singing. They stayed out until about 1:00 that night celebrating and socializing. Adam brought Sara home and she was glad to be snuggled up with Jacob for the rest of the night. She was happy with her new baby and her new romance; they helped keep her mind off the scary problem in her brain.

Adam was around a lot and it was obvious that he was falling in love with Sara *and* Jacob. Most guys would have been spooked by a four month old in a relationship, but not so for Adam . . . not even with the medical problems.

January brought on more tests for Sara. After a neuro-angiogram and other neurological tests, they were told this area of her brain controlled her motor skills, speech, comprehension, memory, cognitive function, etc. . . . basically everything! She and her family were sent home with the news that would challenge the champion of positive thinkers. Faith kept them together and kept them strong as they waited for God to inspire the specialists to decide the next step. Meanwhile, she remained at *high risk* for a brain hemorrhage. The family had already dealt with one of these this past year and it was too fresh to brush off as "oh well, she'll be OK." Mrs. Watson's flash back to her sister's sudden death made it really tough on her. It was hard to even carry on the normal daily duties of life.

At home Sara was taking on the most important role of her life. She was a *wonderful* mom to Jacob; dedicated to spending every possible minute loving, cuddling, talking to him and teaching him things. Her parents loved their role as grandparents and were a tremendous help. Her sister-in-law would sometimes keep him when she worked days since she was home with Elizabeth and Edward. One day Sara said to her, "You know, it's crazy how we can go on about our daily lives as if nothing is wrong while we wait for answers. I try not to think about it, but how can you not with so much at stake?" Jennifer replied, "God Sara, I don't know how you do it. You always seem so together!" "Prayer and faith!" Sara said as she got Jacob ready to walk out the door. "See you guys later."

Mrs. Watson didn't just wait for answers, she educated herself via Internet, books, and medical publications; studying any material she could find to help understand what her daughter would be going through.

The answers came, but not what they were hoping for. During the next appointment at Barnes, the doctor said, "It has been concluded that the problem area in her brain is *inoperable*, proven so by the last neurological test results." "In addition, during the testing, we found another area of concern", he said as he looked at her mom. ("What? What else?" she wondered.) "Between the two frontal lobes of her brain lies an aneurysm about two inches back between her eyes." Looking back at Sara, "This area is of smaller concern, but it dictates how we handle the bigger issue." He went on to explain an AVM, the dangers, and the treatment.

He started out with, "As I described before, an AVM, or Arterio-Venous Malformation, is an abnormal group of blood vessels. As our bodies are designed, the lungs oxygenate the blood (which is red) and it's pumped by the heart through arteries to the brain where it enters a fine network of tiny vessels, called capillaries. It is in these capillary beds where the blood nourishes the tissues with nutrients including oxygen. Deoxygenated or blue blood then passes back to the heart through veins. An AVM is a mangled area that lacks the tiny capillaries but attaches the arteries and veins with a shunt. It can be thought of as a "short circuit" where blood does not go to the tissues, but is pumped through the shunt and back to the heart without ever giving vital nutrients to the tissues. This leaves the blood with a high level of oxygen, therefore, in an AVM the flow is high and the pressure is elevated in the veins." The family sat still trying to take in all this medical info and commit it to memory as he continued! Whew!!

"Studies, up to now, have not been conclusive on exactly what causes an AVM," he said. "Some may form due to a problem with a blood vessel during development before a person is born. It does *not* appear to be inherited." Sara's mom spoke, "My younger sister died earlier this year from a massive brain hemorrhage." "Is that just *coincidental*?" she asked. "I have no answer for you in this case, Mrs. Watson," he seemed to apologize.

There was a pause and then he continued, "The obvious danger of an AVM is the strain on blood vessels and surrounding tissues. Weakened vessels can rupture which is called a hemorrhage, as you said, or a *bleed*. If this happens, as with your sister . . . I'm so sorry to say, the patient commonly has a stroke or often doesn't make it. Even without a bleed, a large AVM can cause progressive neurological problems by putting pressure on the brain or altering blood flow."

*Inoperable* was the doctor's word that kept going over and over in their heads as they listened to his recommended actions. "In your case, Sara," he said, "with that area of your brain controlling several functions; radiation is our *only option*. The recommended plan is to use a relatively new piece of equipment called the Gamma Knife. There will be several shots of radiation from different angles under the direct supervision of several specialists. The goal is, over time, to completely obliterate the AVM to protect her from the possible bleed." Mr. Watson spoke, "You said over time. How long 'til she's safe?" The doctor answered, "Two years is the time frame and then it may need to be repeated if it's not totally gone. Until then she will continue to be at risk, I'm sure that's not what you were wanting to hear." Her dad said, "No sir, it wasn't! And what about the aneurysm?" (Sara is just sitting there trying to take this all in . . . too blown away to even ask anything!) "We sometimes see these along with an AVM because of the strain on the blood vessels," the doctor said, "I'm sorry, this is another reason why hers is inoperable; if we worked on one area, it could cause the other to rupture. I feel the Gamma Knife is the right choice; we have had remarkable success with this procedure in other cases. Sometimes the aneurysm will diminish along with the AVM. I do need to point out there can be significant side effects from the radiation, but *insignificant* to the alternative." He asked, "Is this alright with you, Sara?" She shook her head in agreement . . . at a loss for words. "I'll have my assistant come in, she'll set-up the appointment right away for the pre-op exam and the procedure. She will tell you what to expect that day." He shook Mr. Watson's hand first, then shook Sara's and also put his other hand over hers, as if to be reassuring her this was the right choice.

After she made the appointments and told her what to expect, the assistant asked Sara if she was nursing the baby. Then she went on to tell her that the radiation would be harmful and she *could not nurse afterward.* The young lady felt like she had been stabbed in the heart! One of the greatest joys of being a new mother was nursing her baby.

This appointment had given them a few things to talk about on the way home. Some of the facts about an AVM they already knew due to the research they had done; but when your physician presents it to *you personally* in greater detail, it really hits home.

Jennifer had kept Jacob while they went to the appointment. By the time they got home Sara's breasts were reminding her that he hadn't nursed in a while. Any mother that has nursed knows exactly how that feels, a wonderful feeling yet sometimes painful. Today was especially painful physically and emotionally. She really couldn't believe that he would no longer be able to take her breast milk after the procedure. She nestled her baby into her chest, tears streaming down her face, and rocked him as he nursed.

The next day she started preparing for the changes. Their plan was to wean him off breast milk and on to a recommended infant formula. *Her plan* had been to nurse as long as possible since she was producing an abundant amount of milk and because it's so good for his development. She tried to think positive and was thankful he had already gotten a few months of her nourishment and antibodies. After every formula feeding she would express a bottle full to freeze for later. He handled the alternating between nursing and bottle really well. The little guy still just liked to eat!

The next few days they all tried to go about their daily lives with work and caring for the children. All the news lately was so hard to accept, but again they were so *very thankful* that this problem was found before anything worse happened, thanking God every day for that blessing.

## Chapter 10

# The Gamma Knife

February 17th was the date for the Gamma Knife treatment. Jacob stayed with his Aunt Jennifer again; Adam went along with Sara and her parents. The trip took almost two hours, so they talked about everything possible to keep her mind off the procedure. Of course, things about Jacob dominated most of the conversation. He had been sitting up since he was five months old, so the playtime was really getting fun for the whole family. They shared stories and laughs, even ones they could laugh about now but not quite so funny at the time; like how he would cry for Sara when she went back to work. The only thing to get him to settle down or sleep was to go for a ride in the car. Her mom and dad went for way too many rides before they thought about keeping the stroller in the house. He would ride totally quiet until the wheels stopped and then there came the wails! When they would get him all the way to sleep at night, they'd leave him in the stroller until she got home. A crying baby can be exhausting, especially for grandparents. That period didn't last long, thank goodness. He got used to being without her some and was a lot more fun for everybody. He was an excitable, and vocal little guy. You could already tell he was going to be an extrovert...and probably a *talker*, like his mommy.

Conversation and laughs diminished, as they got closer to Barnes Hospital. The pre-op tests had been done so they were ready for her pretty soon after she arrived. When she was called back, everyone else was asked to remain in the waiting room. Mom and Dad both hugged her and assured her she was in good hands. She reached out for Adam's hand and he pulled her in for a hug.

When in the prep room, the tech asked, "Miss Sara, you've been informed about this, right?" She answered, "Yes . . . but I'm still scared." He assured her the screws were the hardest part, but he would numb the areas as much as possible. Just the anesthetic needle made tears stream down her sweet face. But she soon found out that the injections were NOTHING compared to the screws!! Her tears turned into ANGUISH as two techs on opposite corners inserted screws into her skull *simultaneously* in order to hold her head steady; then did it a second time for the *other two screws*. SHE FELT ANY MINUTE SHE WOULD PASS OUT FROM THE PAIN! It was almost *unbearable*, harder than childbirth that was, up to now, the toughest pain she had ever endured! They were finally finished attaching the halo and she was left with a major headache. They gave her Tylenol to help take the edge off; but it would not take effect for a while.

Just when she expected them back for the procedure, her doctor came in with some surprising news. "Sara," he began, "We won't be able to do the Gamma Knife today."

"But why?" she wondered. "Your pre-op blood test shows you are *pregnant.*" She would have *fainted* to the floor if she hadn't already been sitting down. Her mind raced . . . "We only made love once . . . how can this be happening to me?" She looked up at the nurse with her hands shaking in a praying position over her mouth and could barely speak, "Would you please get Adam?" She nodded and left the room. Sara and the doctor didn't say a word to each other. She kept her hands to her mouth saying under her breath, "Oh my God, Oh my God, Oh my God!"

The nurse went to the waiting room and asked Adam to come back; then she turned to her parents and said, "Something showed up in her blood work and we can't go ahead with the procedure today." Of course, her parents worried about what could be wrong and why she asked for Adam and not one of them.

When Adam got to her room, he felt his heart pounding in his chest when he saw her tears and the thing attached to her head. He fell to his knees beside her as she whispered in a frail voice, "*I'm pregnant.*" "*What*?" he whispered back. They both wept as the doctor explained the radiation would kill the baby, and that was not a decision the hospital was prepared to make. "You both need to give this some serious thought, having this baby will most likely put your life in *significant danger*," he said. "I'm not in a position to tell you what to do, but, if you choose to terminate, an abortion out of *medical necessity* could be performed," he continued, "then this procedure can be rescheduled." He softly said, "God be with you", as he left them alone.

Adam squeezed her tight around her waist and laid his head in her lap as he cried harder. He looked up and said, “Marry me, I’ll stand beside you. We’ll get through this together . . . say you’ll *marry me*!” “Yes . . . I will,” she promised, as they kissed through the tears!

They were allowed a few minutes to digest the news that was just delivered; then the techs came back to remove the screws. They agreed not to tell their parents quite yet; they needed time to decide what to do first. Not much was said on that two-hour trip home. Sara slept from sheer exhaustion. When she got home, snuggling up with Jacob’s little body and being *thankful* for him was all she could think about.

The following morning she told Adam she had to tell her mom the reason for halting the procedure and what the doctor told them. Mrs. Watson was shocked and heartbroken for her daughter. She and Adam had to make a decision of a lifetime. Do they risk her life and have the baby, or do they take away the life their new love had created? This was going to take some serious prayer time.

They both sat down with their parents and discussed the baby, the dilemma it had created, and the decision they had to make. Each one expressed their opinion; none of them were for abortions in general. She checked with her insurance and they would cover an abortion of “medical necessity”, when the *mother’s life was at stake*.

Mrs. Watson immediately started talking to every medical professional she could get to listen, and asking their opinion. The consensus was “to consider the health of the mother first”. The known risk of an AVM is great enough; adding pregnancy and childbirth magnifies that risk! "Jacob needs his mother, please take all this into consideration!" she pleaded with them.

Adam said to her a couple days later, "This is my first baby," (putting his hand on her stomach) ". . . but, without you it would be unbearable. We have to do it." Tears welled up again as they looked at each other. This was the most painful decision either of them had ever made. "Ok," she said hugging Jacob, "I'll set up the appointment tomorrow, *God forgive us!"*

"Tell me again that you'll marry me!" Adam pleaded as he reached in his pocket and got down on one knee. "Yes, of course I will; nothing has changed that," Sara said softly, putting her hand to his face while holding Jacob on her right hip. He kind of half way smiled and said, "Good, because I just financed this thing." He took her left hand and placed a gorgeous one-carat engagement ring on her finger. She looked at her hand and said, "You did good . . . *really* good." Then she kissed him with tears streaming down her cheeks and whispered, "I love you and I know we're doing the right thing."

Both families were relieved; everyone knew she was in eminent danger at any time. Just days before the appointment though, she *miscarried* and it was not discussed openly afterward. Sara and Adam seemed to handle it very well, even though it broke their hearts. Sara would sit at quiet times and wonder what it would look like. Was it a boy or a girl? Green or brown eyes? And would I have survived? She would always wonder and forever be changed, but she felt content that it was the right thing to have happened. Somehow her faith was letting her know that it was well with God.

The Gamma Knife Radiation was rescheduled two weeks later. This time Sara's mom stayed home with Jacob; Sara, Adam, and Dad would make the trip. She was even more apprehensive today because she knew how bad the screws were going to hurt, even though they were the least invasive of today's procedure. All the way there, the guys tried to keep her mind on other things. Again they talked and laughed about the fun things Jacob was doing as he grows. The stages go so fast at that age you'd almost have to document them to remember them all. They pondered the relationship with his cousin, Edward, being so close in age. Sara exclaimed, "They're only a few months old and already have distinct differences in appearance and personality, Jacob blonde, Edward brown, Jacob boisterous, Edward gentle . . . ah, it'll be fun to watch 'em grow up!" Dad said a silent prayer, "God *please* let her see them grow up", as a lump appeared in his throat. He and Adam exchanged glances as if to say "Amen".

She was on time for her appointment and reluctantly followed the tech when he called her name. She said with a frown, as she looked back over her shoulder at Dad and Adam, "Maybe I don't want to be Sara Watson today!" They waved to her and both said, "I love you", at the same time.

The techs were very kind and again apologetic for the pressure they had to use to attach the halo to her head. This time was different . . . she knew how bad it was going to be and prepared herself for it mentally. Tears welled up in her eyes again just remembering the last time and what had to happen. After it was securely attached, they had her lie down on the bed of this large machine that looked very high tech. They asked her to lie very still when instructed.

Dad was pacing and saw them taking her back. He followed carefully, trying not to get too close. When her doctor saw him, he invited him to come back and observe through a window. It was heart breaking for him to see his *little girl* lying there with that big halo screwed into her head. He was never one to like taking the kids to the doctor or watch anything they had to get done. He was pretty squeamish about stuff like that; he would always politely excuse himself.

Her neurosurgeon repeated what to expect. The equipment was amazing, very impressive. Several specialists were in another room with the computer controls. He could see them as they all discussed and contemplated on each tiny spot, angle, intensity, etc. When all the great minds agreed, the tech asked her to take a breath and hold it . . . then the button was pushed to administer the radiation. The objective was to kill out the AVM vessels while preserving the functions of the brain. Her life was in their hands and many prayers were being said for God to guide them. The treatment was complete after *eleven intense bolts of radiation!* The screws and halo were removed and she was released with a bad headache, but ready to get a hug from Dad and Adam!

The doctor consulted afterwards, "Remember, the radiation itself can cause side effects on all the functions of the brain that were affected. Also, this takes a long time, up to two years and then may have to be repeated." He warned, "As we've already discussed, until the AVM is obliterated, she will *continue to be at high risk for a bleed.*" He shook hands with all three of them, and said "God Bless" to Sara. They headed home optimistic that at least the healing process had begun.

## Chapter 11

# Side Effects

Jacob was again the first thing on her mind when she got home. He was all smiles, as usual . . . just to see her face! What a fun stage he was in; he would jump in his seat, squeal and hold both arms up as soon as he saw her. Of course by now he was saying several audible sounds that the whole family enjoyed.

When morning came, Mrs. Watson witnessed the first side effect. Sara sat up in bed and said *"sleep he night good"* and a few other *incomprehensible sounds!* She got a surprised look on her face that turned into a giggle. "Ahhh, what was that?" she squealed. "I meant he had a good night's sleep." Then with a worried look she said, "Do you think that's what they meant about side effects?" Not giving her mom a chance to answer, she cried, "Oh my gosh, mom . . . TALKING IS MY JOB!! "Hey, it'll be OK, honey," assured her mom, "we'll check with the doctor. " Sara went on taking care of Jacob as her mom went straight to Mr. Watson about what just happened. "Call the doctor right away," he said, "and if we're not satisfied, we'll get other opinions, simple as that." He then hurriedly said good-bye and left for work. He already had the name of a famous brain surgeon in Phoenix, Arizona, just in case they needed another opinion!

Mom watched the clock and called the neurosurgeon's office right around 9:00. She told the nurse what had happened and asked to speak with the doctor. The nurse answered that it wasn't necessary and that she could go over more possible side effects. She repeated some that they had already heard, but at the time they weren't worried about side effects; they were just concerned about saving her life! She said Sara could lose some memory; speech could be affected, as she witnessed this morning; and she could lose some hair on that side of her head. Think of these things as a trade off while we're trying to get rid of the serious health risk. Sara was on the extension and heard every word! Her mom heard a gasp as she was hanging up the phone, so she hurried into the other room. "It'll be OK . . . we'll get through this," she whispered as she hugged her daughter and grandson. "Oh, dear God", she prayed silently, "Please heal my precious daughter!"

Before having Jacob, Sara would have been more concerned about her hair. But instead, as tears rolled down her cheeks, she cried, "I don't want to forget *any minute* of my time with *him!*" "We'll do everything we can and pray to keep that from happening," said her mom as she cried with her daughter.

They took lots of photos and videos, and then reviewed them often to keep things fresh in her memory. He was such a blessing to her life; he brought endless hours of smiles and laughter.

A couple weeks later, while brushing her hair Sara yelled, "MOM!" Mrs. Watson wondered how many times had she heard *that yell* this past year? She hurried into the bathroom to see a big hunk of hair in Sara's hand. "Oh, sweetheart . . . let me see," she said lifting her daughter's beautiful hair to see a large oval shaped bald spot at the radiation site. "Maybe that's it" she assured, "this could be *all* you lose." Sara breathed out, "I hope so!" After looking at it in the mirror a few more seconds she said, "Hey, it doesn't look too bad if I'm careful how I pull it back." She couldn't pull it back tight, but loosely it covered the spot. This was how she wore her hair most of the time anyway, in a ponytail or a bun with little strands of hair hanging down, softly framing her face.

Sara was tough about all this; she didn't let it interfere with her daily responsibilities of caring for Jacob and tried not to let it affect her duties at work. It took a toll emotionally of course. But, she woke up every morning *thankful*, even when Jacob didn't let her get much sleep.

She got through the next few months with only small side effects. Any pain in that side of her head got immediate attention, knowing the continuous risk of a bleed. A clash with a female supervisor at work happened when she accused her of *using* her health issue to miss work! She had put in several years with the company and was very disappointed at that accusation. She said life was too short to work for someone with an attitude like that, so she quit. She took a little time off, but knew she had to start looking for a company with good health insurance, considering the things at hand.

God helps things happen for the faithful. It just so happened that the company Mrs. Watson worked for had decided to add another sales rep for the area. The company was Welcome Wagon; the position was selling advertising to businesses for an address book that was sent to new homeowners. If they were going to split the area between two reps, why not keep it in the family. She interviewed and landed the job! This is a young woman with no outside "face to face" sales experience.

She studied the company and what her responsibilities were then went out and nailed it! It was her smart natural ability to present the program and close the sale that made her successful. Her customers were patient with her speech when she briefly explained what she'd been through; and she would make them laugh as she joked about her memory requiring her to "write everything down". The company honored her hard work with great compensation. They also had the insurance coverage that she needed so urgently. It was part of a master plan that God had orchestrated! From the supervisor that made her leave her job, the timing of this company "deciding" to add another rep, the great income, the freedom to be a mom and plan a wedding, and the wonderful insurance coverage . . . what a Godsend!

## Chapter 12

# Wedding Plans

There were a few bumps in the road, but pretty much smooth sailing as she dealt with the changes in her life. She and Adam had chosen a September 2000 wedding date. They imagined, as did many other couples, that the first year in the 21st century would be special! The church and reception hall were secured first, then they could relax and work on the remaining details.

Adam's mom had a "hissy fit" about the short notice; she wondered how in the world they could plan an elaborate wedding in eight months! Sara's attitude was "watch me!" But in the back of her mind she thought, "If my health doesn't get in the way".

Her new job was a perfect fit. The two reps shared the ten county area covering Southeast Missouri and Southern Illinois; and since they were a mother/daughter team, there was no controversy over who got which account. They made a great team! For a while, one worked from home watching Jacob, while the other was in the field. They stayed in touch by phone passing on leads and contact information until he was a little older, then Sara thoroughly checked out daycare options. She knew right away if one was not for her, from stinky facilities to undesirable personnel. Finally, she found one, Tendercare, owned by a former classmate's parents and really liked the atmosphere, teachers, philosophy, etc. The only thing she didn't like so much was the fee, but confidence of the care received outweighed the concern.

When they started traveling together, the wedding plans really kicked into gear. Between appointments, they would slip into bridal shops and try on everything in her size. The theme and invitations were plotted after weeding out several styles of dresses. Sara had determined that the theme would be *fairy tale*, which was easy on invitations, but the dress had to be "the one", without a doubt. Invitations chosen for this theme had a castle and a carriage on the front that read, "Dreams do come true!" and inside "Our wedding will be a fairy tale . . . a dream without end." Her mom then found a poem and reworded it some to fit Sara and Adam, then had it printed along with the invitations.

One day, at a small downtown shop in Cape Girardeau, she found it, the "*perfect*" dress. It was an ivory halter top with beautifully designed lace and a feminine old-fashioned fitted waistline then went out into a full flowing skirt and long train.

She put it on and walked out to the viewing area with several mirrors and a platform to step onto. She threw her hair up in a quick bun. After a long admiring gaze in the mirror, looking at all angles of the gown; she put her hands over her heart, looked at her mom, and said, "This is it! The ONE!" Then asked, "Do you like it, mom?" Tears welling up in her eyes, Mom shook her head and said, "Oh Sara, . . . you look like a *princess*!" She had been biting her tongue since she walked out of the dressing room to *not say a word* until Sara expressed her opinion; she didn't want to influence her at all; she had to really *love it* herself. She lifted the train and went into a swirl before heading back to the dressing room.

Sara said softly, "Mom, this is more than I was planning to spend on my dress . . .but it's so perfect!" She looked in the mirror one more time before taking it off. "I agree wholeheartedly and it's the *only one* in the shop...it's *meant* to be," her mom agreed. "But . . ." Sara started as she was interrupted. "Surely you didn't think we'd leave this *all* up to *you*!" smiled her mom. Sara gave her a hug with a deep sigh as tears rushed in.

She got dressed then went back to discuss the details. The shop owner took them into her office, which was elegant décor down to the beautiful chairs they sat in. Mrs. Watson spoke first, "The dress is a little more than she was planning to spend. Could you take half today and let us pay the rest in a couple months?" The lady said, "Yes, ma'am, most of the gowns in my shop are sold this way. But, here is the rule I have to enforce, the first half is forfeited if you don't finish paying the balance." Sara spoke up, "Well, there's this thing with my health that may cause a delay, but I don't foresee a cancellation." She quickly said, "Of course, exceptions are made for extenuating circumstances. But, let's don't go there...have faith you'll see this wedding thru." They all agreed and continued with the necessary details of the wedding and deadlines. Adam was responsible for picking out the style of tux, and then the guys were to just drop by for tux fittings...no appointments needed.

As they left the shop, Sara said softly, "This is really *happening*...I just bought a *wedding dress*!" Then she let out an "Ahhh!" shaking her hands. They both laughed and started talking accessories.

She found the perfect headpiece on a shopping trip to St. Louis. The lady with the dress said she could do what ever headpiece Sara chose and would add the tulle for the veil the exact length desired and however the bride wanted it attached. One more thing checked off the list of "to do's".

The shoes were a different story; she exhausted every store within a 100-mile radius. In between appointments, she would ask business owners to direct her to the shoe stores in town. She finally went online and found *ivory* strap heels with *rhinestones*! Perfect for her dress! She didn't have a credit card, so she had to walk out on the front porch where Dad was and plead her case. Of course, he said OK and pulled out his credit card. She gave him a quick hug and said, "I'll pay you back." But, he didn't *hold* his *breath* on that one. She hurried back to the computer and placed her order. When they came in a few days later, they fit *exactly* like she had imagined and the ivory color matched. These shoes were keepers and well worth the price of $78.

## Chapter 13

# Summer & More Planning

As the summer months came about, there were more family gatherings in Grandma and Grandpa's backyard. Grandma loved and cared for the flowers, but Grandpa was the one to keep the two acres mowed and trimmed neat for the grandkids.

Elizabeth was really growing and loved helping with her little brother, Edward. One day, Sara asked her if she would like to be her flower girl. She was thrilled and ran over and gave Sara a big hug.

Grandma bought her a Precious Moments book about a wedding day so they could read about her role for that day. She loved reading to her Granddaughter and Grandpa did too, especially when she would fall asleep on his lap.

Grandpa also loved carrying around both boys while they were small enough to carry one on arm each. He got to spend more time with Jacob since he lived with them. As he got bigger, he carried him around the yard on his shoulders. He taught him to appreciate flowers, to be gentle with the petals and enjoy the smell. "Take time to smell the flowers" . . . that was *exactly* what the Watson family was doing this summer.

The Taylor family had an above ground pool with an elaborate deck built around it that was a favorite place this time of year. Sara and Jacob were invited over often; Jacob loved the pool. He started walking early that summer, before he was 10 months, and was a bundle of joy! Adam's parents loved Jacob and were wonderful with him. She even had thoughts of how good a family they would be for Jacob if anything happened to her.

Sara's dad was crushed when she informed him that she and Adam were getting an apartment together and moving before the wedding. Adam was stepping in as Jacob's dad, which was inevitable and a potential blessing for Jacob. Grandpa knew the day was coming and eventually got over it. He later said, when Adam and Jacob were playing and laughing, "I was *once* his favorite."

In the midst of work, babies, gardening, golf, swimming and planning a wedding that summer; there was something else brewing, something other than Sara's brain. One July morning, her mom got a call from Aunt Sue. Her pap test had come back positive for cervical cancer! She was *really close* to her sister and this hit hard. She and Uncle Lee were always at their family holiday dinners . . . always buying them presents at birthdays and Christmas.

Mrs. Watson held it together pretty good until the whole body P.E.T. scan showed *cancer active* in all her pelvic lymph nodes. "No," she cried when she got the news, "This can't be happening; she's supposed to grow old with me!" She cried herself to sleep that night as she recalled the pain of loosing her mother-in-law, a woman she loved as her own mother, to this horrible disease. She also remembered the pain and suffering her sister-in-law, Carolyn, went through with colon cancer and *won* the fight. "God, please let my sister *win* the *fight*!" she prayed as she went off to sleep.

Hearts were torn in all different directions in this "turn of the century" year. Sue had to go through six weeks of daily chemo and *internal* radiation at Barnes Hospital. She was allowed to stay at Ronald McDonald's house, which was near the hospital, during the week and then she could come home on weekends. Sue's mom, Sara's grandmother (Mama), left her home responsibilities in Mississippi to stand by her daughter's side the whole six weeks. There was no reservation at all; when she heard the news about her daughter, she couldn't imagine being anywhere else.

Some weekends her grandmother would stay with her parents, to give Aunt Sue and Uncle Lee some alone time. Sara's mom wanted to keep the atmosphere positive, so she suggested doing craft projects for the wedding. Aunt Sue and Mama worked on tissue box covers in ivory yarn with lace and beads, as they passed time between treatments each day. Sue didn't feel great but her body handled it better than she expected and she didn't lose any hair.

Sara's mom worked on items every free minute she'd get. She had read somewhere that the ring bearers of long ago used boxes instead of pillows. This would be great for the little one year old that had the honor . . . yes, Jacob was to be the ring bearer for his mom and "dad's" wedding! He would be one by then.

Mrs. Watson found a small wooden box at a local craft store that looked like a little treasure chest. She covered and lined it with ivory satin and lace. (Easier said than done!) Then, one night while working at the dinner table, she looked up at the china cabinet and saw something special they could use. It was a small ivory *porcelain* basket that Aunt Sue sent with flowers when Sara was born. It was 23 years old and in perfect condition for the flower girl's basket. Ivory lace was hot glued around the top edge and a delicate matching flower on one side where the handle met the basket. Sue would be proud to have her basket used in the wedding. "Wow, check off one more beautiful thing for her special day!" she said to her husband who was stretched back watching TV. "It's *really* beautiful, Mom," he said. (They had called each other "Mom" and "Dad" since Wayne and Sara were little.) There was something uniquely emotional about the preparation of their only daughter's wedding. (And her medical condition certainly didn't make things any easier for them.)

Sara had chosen sage to go with the ivory for her wedding color scheme...now the very important decision of bridesmaids' dresses. Her maid of honor was Wayne's wife, Jennifer; bridesmaids were Debra, (Jennifer's sister-in-law) and Katy (Adam's sister). She was determined to choose a style that would flatter all their figure types. They were all pretty girls with nice figures, so it wasn't going to be a hard task. The day they found the perfect dress she was shopping with her mom and Jennifer. They had gone from store to store trying dresses on Jennifer as their model. She had on a beautiful sage dress that fit her perfectly when she blurted out, “Sara, guess who’s pregnant?” “Not you!" Sara screeched. “Lord NO,” answered Jennifer, "It's Debra!” The shop owner spoke up quickly answering the question already in Sara’s mind. “This dress is easy to work with” she assured, “all we have to do is order extra material and do a fitting two weeks prior to insert the panels.” “Whew, that’s great” sighed Sara, “OK, this *IS* the *dress*!” It was a *flattering* style with spaghetti straps, fitted at the bust line and toward the waist then flared slightly to flow beautifully...not one of those confining dresses at all. To add to the elegance, she ordered the matching shawl made of sheer sage material.

They all enjoyed shopping for items to match the shade of green; it’s amazing how many shades of sage are out there. All the laughs with the wedding plans made them sometimes forget, even for a few minutes, about the mess of blood vessels in her brain and her aunt’s fight with cancer. It was good medicine.

Jacob was growing fast that summer and he was so much fun! They did trial runs with him walking with a small box in his hands to practice for the wedding. He was already walking great, so Sara thought he should be fine with it. He would do it sometimes in practice, but most of the time he’d drop the box and come running to her with a great big smile! What more can you expect from a little guy? When they took him to be fitted for his tux, the lady said he was definitely the *smallest* she’d ever measured.

His first birthday was one of great celebration and praise. Here he was, the boy the doctor said was not going to make it, all *happy*, *handsome*, and *healthy*! His was a life to be thankful for as they recognized the miracle of prayer for him and Sara. She used her natural artistic ability and drew Mickey Mouse, his favorite cartoon character, on his customized party invitations. Mickey, with one finger up, turned out so cute, she used the design on his cake too. Family and friends showered him with cards and presents. Sara felt blessed with their expression of love.

The wedding plans continued each week of the summer. Sara's mom started saving rose petals from her garden for the flower girl's basket. When time grew closer, she started asking other gardeners to donate. One day when Elizabeth was with her, they went by the Rose Garden in a nearby town. They picked up petals that had fallen, which was OK with the park department. But when she still needed a few more, she walked back through the roses and *barely* touched ones that were about to fall off anyway, kind of like *helping* them along. They brought all those rose petals home and scattered them out to dry in the living room floor. Dad walked through and said, "Great, now I've got to step over flowers until this wedding?" He sounded agitated, but in his heart he was proud of his daughter for handling everything on her plate so efficiently as they planned out her dream wedding. Cost went through his head but it was only a thought...once in a lifetime, right?

It wasn't easy for Sara and her mom; planning a wedding while pleasing an employer takes a lot of juggling. Both of them set up new customers and even opened up new areas that summer. They were a good team, which was great for all parties. Sara had few symptoms during those months, so they all prayed the radiation was doing its *thing*.

The family gave her a bridal shower in August. The banquet room was already classy so they just decorated some in her colors. Several family members and friends lavished her and Adam with lots of nice things to help start their new life together. A relative of Adam's even traveled from Chicago to be here for the occasion.

One of the games was designing a wedding dress out of toilet paper on a live model. There was laughter that could be heard all over the facility. The winner was pretty clever; Jean & Lorie were a mother/daughter team (friends her parents had known since their first year of marriage). They must have played the game before, because in the time allowed, they not only created a full wedding dress but also a TP veil. It was a fun shower. Sara was proud that her Aunt Sue and Mama were able to be there. Sue's treatments were done and she was holding her own as she dealt with a lot of abdominal pain. She was just happy to be there for Sara.

The week of the wedding, Mom and Dad were sitting on the front porch talking about some details. An elaborate affair had been planned, much more than anticipated early on. Even so, Dad spoke up and said, "There's one more thing I have to do for her." Mom pondered what in the world he was thinking, as she shook her head and smiled. "What?" she asked. "I want to surprise her with a limo at the end of the evening, so Adam won't have to drive." They were very lucky to find one available at such a late date. The cost was $100 paid in advance, which included iced-down Champaign and a drive around town before driving them to their hotel. They were surprisingly able to keep the secret!

Two days before the wedding, Sara took her mom with her to get a pedicure and manicure. She had never had a pedicure and it was Sara's treat for all she had done. They went to the spa in the afternoon after a productive day of work. "Oh, man . . .this is amazing!" her mom said referring to the warm soak. She had Fibromyalgia and dealt with *overall body pains*, so this was a real treat for her feet! The spa offered a glass of Champaign as they relaxed. They talked about wedding details to make sure they hadn't forgotten something important. The way they talked and laughed, it was obvious they were more than mother/daughter; they were *best friends.* As they walked out, Sara did a shoulder bump and giggled, "I told you you'd love it, Mom". Mrs. Watson hooked arms with her daughter and said, "Thank you, sweetheart." She felt pampered and relaxed but kind of like calm before the storm.

Sara had to stop by and get a little color with a spray tan before the big day. Mom just waited in the lounge; she got enough color working in the flower gardens. Their *girl time* was almost up; it was about time to pick up Jacob at daycare.

Sara always liked picking him up before the big after school rush. When they got to the daycare, her mom stood back and watched Jacob to see when he would notice Sara. He was playing with a set of blocks building a tall tower. When he saw his mom, the tower crumbled and he came running with his arms reaching up! Sometimes he would be so happy to see her he would start crying.

Sara had picked up his tux earlier, so when they got to their apartment she tried it on. It was a struggle to get him in it; he was too excited to be home. "Oh, how cute!" "Couldn't get any cuter!" said her mom, "I've got to get home and start supper. Hugs & kisses...see ya tomorrow; but *we are NOT working*." Sara handed her mom a note when she was leaving. "Wait 'til you get home to read it...we'll practice carrying that box!" promised Sara, as she waived good-bye with Jacob on her hip.

Mrs. Watson couldn't wait to open her note, it read . . . "One of the million things I love about you is that you are always so tough about your pain. If it gets you down, you never show it. Like I've said before, you make me want to be a better person just from watching you. You're a great role model, an amazing mother and friend. I used to say, "When you go, we go together because I never want to live without you." But now I have Jacob and can't say that anymore; now I understand how you feel about me as your child. He is such a part of me that I can't imagine life without him either. If anything happens to me, I want you to stay an important part of his life . . . teach him your values. Thank you for being the good person that you are and thank you for loving me so unconditionally. I love you, Momma!"

Tears were streaming down her face when she finished reading. "Nothing can happen to *you*, sweetheart; my *heart* couldn't take it", she said out loud as she started her car to head home.

## Chapter 14

# Wedding 2000

September 2, 2000 was almost upon them. The weather was perfect, very warm with calm winds. They went over last minute details one more time and checked off things that were completely ready. The reception hall could not be decorated until after the rehearsal dinner. That made Sara a little nervous. When they were first told of this rule it didn't seem to present a problem; but now that it was a day away . . . hmmm. Would they have time, or enough help, to get it done at a reasonable hour?

The dinner went well, everyone was able to attend. The reservation was at Delmonico's, a local restaurant. Adam had asked his best man's little sister to be in the wedding too; so she was there with him. Chloe was not much older than Elizabeth, so it worked out great that they got to meet each other the day before. The kids kept the atmosphere cheery which helped, since the in-laws knew nothing about each other.

Sara had planned out every little detail for the reception, drew out the floor plan and decided exactly where the icicle lights were to be hung. She made copies of the plan to give to the friends and relatives kind enough to show up and help.

Immediately after dinner they headed to the reception hall to *transform* it into a luxurious fairy tale reception! To Sara's surprise, several of Adam's friends and relatives from out of town showed up. All she had to do was direct traffic. Her dad got the guys going on moving out the rectangular tables and replaced them with the rented round ones according to the floor plan. The only rectangular ones used were for the food tables and the head table arrangement. The ivory tablecloths were put in place and made the place start to look like a wedding reception. Adam helped hang the lights above the dance floor, across the front of the head tables and around the cake and ice sculpture table. Sara stood back and approved each step as it fell in place. She had chosen round mirrors with ivory candles for the centerpieces. They were very carefully put on each round table. Her mom printed place cards for the head table and close family members' table. The poem she had printed was not shared until now and it read:

*When Sara was a little girl*
*we often used to say,*
*how proud and happy we would be*
*on this her wedding day.*
*Our daughter is not lost to us;*
*in fact, we've gained a son.*
*Adam is her dream come true,*
*today they're joined as one.*
*Their lives are off to a beautiful start*
*with precious memories to share.*
*Our thanks to friends and relatives*
*who came to show you care.*

*Sara & Adam*
*September 2, 2000*

They were rolled up with a gold ring placed around it and put at each setting. One of the tissue boxes that Aunt Sue and Mama had made was put in the ladies bathroom. The only thing left to do was the flowers, food, cake, and castle ice sculpture, which were all scheduled for the next morning. Sara was very pleased as she made a last minute scan of the room...it was already beautiful, even without the flowers! They turned out the lights and left.

Adam's bachelor party was held that night at their new apartment. Sara and Jennifer went by because Sara had forgotten her shoes for the wedding. She said she would only be a minute, so Jen waited in the car. She noticed when Sara came out she had that "OMG" look on her face. "What's wrong?" she asked. "He just called me a *bitch* in front of his friends!" blurted Sara. "Oh shit, Sara...he's just got the pre-wedding jitters" laughed Jen, trying to lessen the hurt. "I hope that's all it is, but I *don't like* it!" Sara said as she spun out of the parking lot and headed for home. They were all spending the night at Mom and Dad's. She was quiet the rest of the way. Jennifer wondered what she was thinking, but decided to let it be . . . Sara would talk when she was ready. That was one thing you could count on, when she had something to say that she was passionate about (like smoking while you're pregnant); there was no stopping her! She remembered once when Sara let her have it big time for smoking while she was pregnant with Edward…not good.

Mom was waiting up for the girls. Everyone else was already asleep. They went into Mom's big bathroom, closed the doors, and plopped down on the cool ceramic tile floor. There was giggles and girl-talk as they thought of everything that still needed to be pulled off by morning. Not counting the things at the reception or the church, but personal things.

All of a sudden, tears welled up in Sara's eyes and she couldn't help a tear running down her cheek. She told her mom what Adam had said to her. "Oh, honey," she assured, "he's probably *nervous* about taking on a wife and a one year old!" "I can pull *my own* weight," cried Sara, "and as for Jacob...I don't see him as a *burden*! Do you think Adam does?" "Sara, you know he loves Jacob," said Jennifer. "I want him to have a dad and extended family in case anything happens to me with this *mess* in my head," Sara continued in a trembling voice, "Is that wrong?" "No, sweetheart," her mom soothed touching her hand, "It's very normal to want your child to be taken care of. We'll all be there for him and so will YOU; I don't think God is done with you yet . . . you have much more to accomplish in life!"

Mom reached out her arms to both girls for a group hug and they said goodnight and went to bed. Sara felt good to be in her old bed snuggled up with Jacob. She whispered a prayer, "Lord, please bless our marriage. I believe I'm making the right decision for Jacob and myself. Please forgive Adam and bless him as he takes on the role of husband and father. Jesus, I hope and pray he's ready."

The morning of the wedding day came too soon after the late night. The children had no mercy for their lack of sleep. Sara's dad made everyone a scrumptious breakfast. He loved to cook, which was a good thing for her mom because she wasn't the greatest. "We all have our strengths and weaknesses," she'd say. Her kids would always say, "Mom's cookin' again!" when they would smell something burning or hear the smoke alarm going off.

After breakfast the women headed to the church for a final check on decorations before they went to get their hair done. Adam's Uncle James was a floral designer and his present to Adam & Sara was to do the flowers for them. He had elegant flowers, greenery, and bows on the candelabras and the church pews. Two huge bouquets were at the alter and one at the guest book. He carried out her ivory and sage theme *beautifully*!

Adam called to meet up with Sara. He apologized for the night before and presented her a wedding gift. It was a beautiful gold and sapphire necklace, which was her birthstone, as well as, the month they were being married. "Oh Adam, it's *gorgeous*!" Sara whispered, "Thank you and I love you." She hugged him hard. "I love you too, Sara; and I promise to do my best!" said Adam before a passionate kiss. "I can't wait to make you my wife! See you this afternoon." "Bye, I'll be there!" she smiled and hurried to the hair salon.

Aunt Sue and Mama were at the guest book by the time Sara and her mom got back to the church. Sue looked great; no one could tell she had been fighting cancer all summer. Mama had on a *pretty* pink dress they had found in St. Louis. Her mom's sister, Sandy, was the only other one able to come from Mississippi. Her dad's family was all coming from out of town, as well as, Adam's out-of-town family. He had a lot of family locally, too. It was going to be a big day!

Sara already looked gorgeous with her hair done up and sporting a country blue checkered button-up shirt and jeans. She did her make-up while Mom and the others got dressed. Then Mom and Jennifer helped her into her gown. She put on her headpiece and veil; it was gathered on to the back portion and draped below her shoulders. She chose to not have any veil over her face. Pearl and diamond dangle earrings; those "perfect" ivory shoes with rhinestones, and a garter belt finished her off . . . what a *princess*! She looked like she just stepped out of a bridal magazine . . . no . . . even better!

Jennifer, Debra, and Katy, looked *beautiful*, too. Debra's dress fit great with the extra panels; it disguised her "baby belly" really well. Katy was a tall blonde and stunning in her own look.

The little girls, Elizabeth and Chloie, were running around with Jacob and playing with Edward in his walker. They had to be tamed a little to avoid a major mishap with their wedding clothes.

It was almost time . . . everyone went upstairs to get into place. Aunt Debbie, Uncle James' wife, stayed behind to help Sara with her dress as she came up the stairs. The church was full and looked so amazing!

Two brothers, Mark and Mike, each sang a beautiful song. They were mutual friends of both families. The candelabra's were then lit without a glitch.

The wedding party entered to "The Wedding Song" by Kenny G at Sara's request. She had always said she wanted to use that song in her wedding someday. Her wish was being granted. Elizabeth and Chloie walked down together, as Elizabeth spread the rose petals she helped gather carrying Aunt Sue's porcelain basket; then they took their place up front with the wedding party. Now it was Jacob's turn . . . everybody was a little apprehensive about this step. He looked so darn cute in the "the smallest tux ever ordered"! Grandpa was the one to get him started, then he went back to be by Sara's side. Jacob went about halfway down the isle with his ring bearer's box; then he stopped cold. Adam squatted down on Jacob's level and coaxed him to come on; but it didn't work. Adam hurried up the isle; he *swooped* him up and carried him to the front! The guests let out a few sighs...it was a precious rescue.

With Adam's nod the organist began to play "The Wedding March", and the priest motioned for everyone to stand. There she was, the most beautiful bride, clinging to her dad's arm as he proudly walked his only daughter down the isle. Mr. Watson was a pretty handsome guy all decked out in his tux. He was proud of his daughter; it showed on his face, even though his hands were shaking at the moment. She gave him a gift before the ceremony; it was a handkerchief that read:

*For Dad,*
*On my wedding day...*
*Your little girl is all grown up;*
*today I'll become a wife!*
*But I know, Dad, that you will always be*
*a very special part of my life.*

Sara's heart was pounding . . . it seemed like a really *long isle* to walk down! And there were *so many* people; she never had so many eyes on her. She couldn't have been happier or more nervous!

Tears had to be fought back when she saw Adam holding Jacob. "He'll be a good dad," she said, and then as she continued down the isle holding on to her dad, she thanked God for all the blessings in her life."

Adam was thinking, "Here comes the *girl* of *my dreams* since high school . . . and she's marrying me!" And he had also fallen in love with the little guy that came along with the package. Sara gave Jacob a kiss as Adam handed him off to her dad.

Before they started their vows, both picked up long-stem red roses and took them to their mothers and grandmothers, delivered with a kiss. (They threw in a surprise on the "wedding planner mom") Mrs. Watson was taken with the gesture and gave her daughter an approving nod with a smile.

Jacob and his cousin, Edward, were to stay with their Grandma and Grandpa for the ceremony. Well, they didn't make it through. It *was* a catholic church and the mass got a little long for them, actually a little long for the grandparents too! Aunt Debbie came down the outside isle and motioned to take both boys to the room in the back of the church. They could see the wedding, but their sounds couldn't disrupt anything. Sara's parents were relieved and were able to appreciate the rest of their daughter's ceremony.

The church was beautiful even without the wedding decorations; the stained glass windows sparkled in the afternoon sun. It was a perfect setting for a formal wedding.

Mrs. Watson's mind wandered as she reflected back on all the months of preparation, her daughter's health risks, and the baby they lost that helped save her life. She prayed, "Thank you God for our daughter, please continue to watch over her and Jacob."

She came back to the present and listened as the bride and groom said their vows. The priest then said, "You may kiss your bride". The tall groom leaned down to kiss his new wife. Then the priest announced, "Ladies and gentlemen, Mr. & Mrs. Adam Taylor!" They hurried up the isle and were followed by the wedding party. After the long receiving line and pictures, the bride and groom surprised the family as they drove off in a borrowed white convertible Mustang.

Adam didn't tell Sara where they were going, but she knew it wasn't the direction of the reception. He pulled up in front of his great-grandmother's nursing home. He called her "Omie". She was there due to her advancing Alzheimer's disease. Even though she didn't always recognize others; she *always knew Adam*! They hurried down the hall drawing lots of attention in their wedding attire. When at Omie's room, she saw him and called out "Big Boy!" which is what she always called him. He gave her a hug and then said, "Omie, I got married today . . . this is my wife, Sara." She smiled and gave Sara a hug.

Meanwhile, all the guests made their way to the reception. The main attraction was the *castle ice sculpture* in the middle of the cake table. Everything looked *so elegant* and the catered food smelled delicious! The guests were patiently waiting the arrival of the bride and groom. Adam told *no one* what he was doing; so everyone wondered where they were.

The photographer, Steve, was an old friend. His wife owned the daycare that Wayne and Sara went to when they were little. Their son, Chris, was the same age as Wayne and their daughter, Lizzy, was a little younger than Sara. Now, Lizzy was all grown up and beautiful, assisting her dad as videographer. Both were ready to catch a snapshot and a video of the bride and groom when they came through the doors.

After arriving, they paused before opening the doors. Adam reached down and kissed her on the forehead and asked, "Ready?" She nodded, and then he said, "Let's do this!" The DJ had been signaled, "Ladies and Gentlemen . . . Sara and Adam!" They quickly came through the double doors holding hands as everyone applauded. They headed straight for the head table giving high-fives and hugs along the way.

After a blessing by Adam's Grandfather, the head table was served their meal, and then the rest of the guests went through the food line. Sara's parents took care of Jacob and made sure he ate. Debra's husband helped with Elizabeth and Edward, but he had two boys to take care of, so they helped with them too. Edward had fun being pushed across the dance floor in his walker. Elizabeth was really good with her brother and she made sure he was not ignored.

Jennifer made the first toast after standing up and clinking her glass, "To Sara and Adam, my sister-in-law deserves the very best; I hope y'all have a long and happy life." Jack, the best man, then stood and said, "I've known you my whole life buddy, you're a good friend and you've found a great gal!" All applauded.

Wayne got up to sing a song for his sister. He liked to sing along with a CD like he did with Jen at their wedding. He started singing but the DJ got the wrong song going . . . so he just went with it, then some of the lyrics were not quite the right message! Wayne had a little smile on his face as he sang, then both he and the DJ apologized when he finished the song...the wedding party chuckled!

The first dance by the bride and groom was announced and they danced to their song, "Amazed" by Lonestar. Sara closed her eyes and remembered how great it felt the first time they danced last New Year's Eve and how she melted in his arms. Her dress flowed beautifully as they swayed to the music. They looked like royalty on the dance floor! Adam kissed his bride again and dipped her back as the song ended. Then she walked over to get her dad for the "Father/Daughter Dance". About half way through, Adam brought his mom to the floor and was joined by Wayne and his mom, then Katy and her dad . . . all four parents dancing with one of the wedding party. That worked out nicely.

Everyone seemed to be having a great time as they danced and visited or just sat back and watched this celebration of love. All the traditional parts of the reception went on without a glitch. The cake cutting was civil, no cake on the face ordeal. They made over three hundred dollars with the dollar dance. The young girls lined up for the bouquet toss; and to Sara's surprise, Alyssa (Adam's x-girlfriend) caught it! Just by being there told that she had forgiven them for the split-up. And besides, she was dating a great guy now. The garter-toss spiced things up a bit when Adam slowly ran his hand up her leg, pretending to not find it. Of course, the DJ went right along with dramatic music.

Sara's dad bowed out early and offered to take Jacob home and put him to bed; the little guy and Grandpa were both exhausted. He hated to miss his limo surprise for his daughter but pictures would have to suffice.

One by one, families came and said good-bye to the couple as the night progressed. When the bride and groom were ready to leave, Steve was ready to capture the surprise. Adam opened the double doors and Sara's jaw dropped! "Ahhh! *A Limo*?" she squealed, as she looked back at her mom puzzled; because she knew they had gone over budget. Mom hugged her and whispered, "From your daddy". His idea accomplished what he wanted . . . his "little girl" to be happy. And the wide-open smile showed she was! One more pose for the camera and they were off.

## Chapter 15

# Honeymoon Horror

Sunday afternoon they gathered at the Taylor's home to open the wedding gifts and document the gifts for thank you notes. Sara still looked *radiant* and *elated*. Jacob was glad to see her; he went running to her with arms up as always. That was the only thing she dreaded about the honeymoon, being away from him for that long!

Going through all the gifts took longer than expected. Their friends and relatives had showered them with so many gifts and envelopes of money. Jacob was just old enough to enjoy getting into the paper and bows, so they just let him be. Her parents were going to keep him while they were gone, after he spent the night with his new grandparents. They were looking forward to him staying over for the first time.

She finished packing special things for their first week as husband and wife; just the right outfits were a necessity of course. They left that evening to drive to Destin, Florida. They were driving straight through taking turns driving and singing with the radio, both too excited to get any sleep. To their surprise, the old song "Going to the Chapel" came on the radio for the second time. Adam acknowledged it and started singing to her as she grabbed the video camera and recorded his performance!

The next morning, just minutes after her parents arrived to pick up Jacob, the phone rang and Mr. Taylor answered. It was Adam! Something had happen to Sara!!

They had been driving all night as planned. About the time the sun was coming up, Adam decided to take a nap. Sara was so excited about getting there, she went ahead and drove while he slept. Suddenly, Adam was startled at a different sound from the wheels going off the road. He looked up and saw her hands on the wheel and a pleasant look on her face as she said, "Something's happening". Her eyes seemed to follow something up and over and she ended up with her head fallen back and hanging over! His instincts took over; he immediately grabbed the wheel avoiding a crash screaming "Sara! Sara!" His long legs reached over from the passenger side to reach the brake and bring the car to a halt. She was unresponsive but jerking in a way he had never seen before! His heart sank; he knew he was losing her. "Sara!" he cried. "God please!" is all he could pray. Other people stopped right away to help and called 911, an ambulance came but a helicopter was brought in when Adam shared her health history. All of them were worried she was *hemorrhaging*. She was being flown to Mobile, Alabama and they wouldn't let Adam ride with her; he was going to have to drive there alone. That's when he made the call home . . .

"Dad!" Adam screamed. "What's wrong son?' he asked. "It's Sara, she's in a freakin' helicopter!" When his dad told everybody it was Sara, her mom yelled, "*WHAT*?" with instant tears flowing. Her dad said, "Calm down, we don't know what's wrong *yet* . . . YOU have to take care of HIM! (nodding to Jacob). She was being told, "not to cry", when their daughter could be dying! Adam's dad tried to relay what he was saying without scaring everybody too badly. Then they all heard Adam scream, "Get down here as soon as you can, I'm freakin' out here!" "We will son . . . you keep it together and get there safe, she needs you," assured his dad. Katy asked for the phone, so he handed it to her.

All their heads were spinning and speculating *what* could be happening and how to get there! Mrs. Watson suddenly remembered, "Steve, our photographer, is a pilot . . . he has his own plane! Both dads simultaneously said, "Call him". She had to look up his number *hands trembling* and *fighting* through tears to see. She quickly dialed the number, "Mary Ann...is Steve home? Something has happened to Sara and we need to get to Alabama ASAP!" "I'll get him," she hurried. Steve came to the phone and asked, "When can you be ready to leave?" "We're at *your mercy,*" Sara's mom said, as she switched to speakerphone. "Be here, I can leave within the hour," Steve responded, "I won't charge for my service, you'll just need to pay for the gas." "No problem," they all agreed. But cost was the last thing on their mind at the moment.

Katy *insisted* on going. "He was begging for me to come . . . he's *going crazy*, he *needs* me!" she pleaded.

It was decided that both dads and Katy would make the trip. Sara's mom stayed home to take care of Jacob. She knew it was most important to be there for him, and that's what Sara would have wanted. The plane trip was a little rough; Katy thought she was going to get sick several times. But they were all glad to get down there quicker than driving. They filled Steve in on what had happened on the way. "It's a miracle that those kids didn't have a major wreck!" he said. Then after an awkward silence . . . he said, "God knew she needed to marry somebody with long legs", trying to lighten the mood a little. "Amen to that!" answered Mr. Watson, shaking his head.

Steve was cleared to land close by the hospital and he asked to have a cab waiting to rush them on over to the ER. He was a good pilot and the plane was a nice one; but its size is what made the flight rough. He gave his blessings to Sara and the family and got back on the plane to return home. They were thankful to have the cab waiting for them. Katy was especially thankful to be on solid ground again.

They hurried to the ER and were directed right to Sara's room. Katy ran to her brother and hugged him tight; he was a wreck! He did not leave Sara's side until the family members got there. He was *so glad* to see them come in. But Sara had *improved* and was *conscious*! She was so *happy* to see her dad that she started crying again! "It'll be OK, Baby", he said as he leaned over and hugged his head up against hers.

After a CT scan and consulting with her neurosurgeon at Barnes, the doctors concluded it was NOT a bleed and that what she had experienced was a *grand mal seizure* while she was driving! Her doctor was surprised that she had gone all summer without incident, since seizures were a side effect after the Gamma Knife. He said *over stimulation* and *exhaustion* probably brought this one on! If there is a tendency toward seizures, extreme stress can make them surface.

"*Not a bleed*" was the part Adam was holding on to and thanking God! Her dad didn't want to let go of her hand. "I'm OK now dad . . .my head hurts but I *don't remember* what happened; I could have *killed us both!*" she cried. "God was watching over you, sweetheart", he whispered as he kissed her hand.

The doctors concluded that she was OK to continue the honeymoon. "Are you kiddin' me . . . for real?" asked Adam. "Even after *all that*?" squeezing her arm. "Yes," said the doctor, "She will have a pretty good headache for a day or two; just keep it *calm* and DON'T let her DRIVE!" That comment brought out a few nervous laughs. Adam smiled and agreed he wouldn't.

Mr. Watson had a real hard time leaving his daughter after that scare; but they headed back home in a rental car for a *long* 12-hour trip, while the bride and groom headed to nearby Destin!

The resort they had chosen was picture perfect. Adam carried her into the bridal suite, closed the door, swirled her around and then gently laid her on the luxurious bed. She held out her hand to stay connected. He started kissing her hand then up her arm. She studied his face, so handsome. As he got to her neck she closed her eyes, then they locked in a kiss of a lifetime. Their clothes must have melted off; because she had no memory of getting undressed . . . just their bodies entangled and becoming one.

The rest of the honeymoon was just as perfect. They both tried to forget the *horror* of its beginning! They took long walks on the beach and swam in the ocean everyday. No jet skis or scuba diving as they had planned, but they were together . . . alone with no interruptions! They had nice romantic dinners every night and long talks afterwards before heading back to their bridal suite. Adam definitely didn't let her out of his sight for one minute.

## Chapter 16

# Another 911 Call

After returning home, the newly weds tried to get things back to normal schedules. The sad part was that the doctor told her she *could not* drive for a *year* after a seizure! The young vibrant wife and mother now had to rely on *someone else* to take her anywhere she needs to go when she was used to her independence.

Sara's mom was, of course, her designated driver most of the time. It was fortunate that she was working from home on her own schedule. Sara was still working for Welcome Wagon *fortunately,* because she had to ask for the short-term disability insurance to kick in until she could drive again. The company was very helpful in getting everything worked out. It really came in handy because Adam's great job that was pending never panned out; he just worked part-time anywhere he could find while he waited.

One day when Sara was drying her hair, she strangely sat down in the hallway and just stared at her mom. She asked, "What are you doin' honey?" Sara couldn't get up or speak but had a sweet and calm expression on her face. She was looking into her mother's eyes, like she had a yearning for her to *read her mind.* She called 911, something wasn't right! Suddenly Sara started calling off four numbers over and over...3219... 3219...3219. Mrs. Watson caught on to what she was trying to say, which was to call Adam at this number! She added the local prefix to those four numbers and found him. He was there *before* the paramedics! He picked her up and gently put her on the bed; then protected her while the seizure took control of his wife again. There was no jerking like a seizure with this episode. Paramedics came and took her to the hospital to check for a bleed, her symptoms were similar to someone having a stroke. She was not able to talk properly and her left arm wouldn't move.

Mom wasn't going to be left behind; she buckled up Jacob and followed the ambulance! Adam was able to ride with her this time.

At the hospital, they ran all the usual tests and determined it was another grand mal seizure. Again, no bleed; thank God. Her high risk just made any episode very scary. The doctors agreed she had to be checked out; but they said she and the family would learn the signs of an *aura*, the pre-seizure feeling, that she would have. Stroke symptoms could be similar but a bleed, or hemorrhage, was usually *very painful*.

Sara returned home and concentrated on being the best mom possible for Jacob. She was so afraid that she might not get to see him grow up. Every playful thing they did together was teaching him something. Jacob soaked up all the info he could! He learned his colors, numbers, shapes, and alphabet like it was just matter of fact. Not much *effort* was needed on his part to retain anything; it all came pretty easily for him. He was such a joy to everyone, but Sara was just *head-over-heels* for her son. She felt that "he" was the reason that God spared her life; she just prayed it would be a *long* life!

While Sara was taking care of Jacob, Mom and Dad did a little more research on their own. Dad pulled out the name of the Neurosurgeon from Phoenix, Arizona. He was famous for his expertise in brain surgery. He was known worldwide; leaders of other countries came to this doctor. When Mr. Watson called his office, he expected the same routine as usual . . . speaking to one person then another. To his surprise instead he was instructed immediately to have Barnes Hospital overnight her records to his office! They had to do the normal formalities of faxing the release for Sara to sign and return before any records could be released.

Within two days there was a response. When his office phone rang, Sara's dad was shocked to hear the doctor introduce himself. He certainly didn't expect that, maybe his assistant or nurse, but not the doctor himself! He went on to explain that his position was the very same . . . it was ***inoperable at this point***. He would be glad to take her as his patient; but he said he would ***not touch*** her until ***two years*** after the Gamma Knife had time to work. That area of her brain controlled too many things to chance it. Barnes was doing the right thing . . . they just had to pray it didn't hemorrhage before then. Mr. Watson thanked him for his time and honest opinion.

Sara knew it was going to be a long haul and she was usually pretty good about needing a chauffeur all the time. There were some days, though, when her mom couldn't get there right away, that she would get angry at her situation. She just wanted to wish it away and jump in the car and run an errand or go grocery shopping! She missed the simple joys of driving herself around; this independent young woman had to totally depend on someone else for the simplest things.

Adam sometimes showed even more anger about her situation, which turned into fits of rage at the flip of a hat. He knew that excessive stress could bring on an episode but seemed to subconsciously forget at times. One night when the doctor had sent her home with electrodes all over her head to record any possible activity, things got out of control with yelling obscenities! Sara was thankful that Jacob was in bed asleep. She didn't recall what started it but was upset and then suddenly felt an aura coming on. She was already sitting on the couch so she picked up the phone and dialed her parent's number. When her mom answered, all she could get out was "Mom!" and then nothing else could be spoken. Her mom heard Adam's voice in the background yelling at Sara; so when she couldn't answer her, she knew something bad was wrong. She hung up and immediately called Adam's dad to get over there quick since he lived closer than they did. She also called the police because it sounded pretty violent and wasn't sure they could get him settled down. Mrs.Watson never shared exactly what she heard him say that night...words she would never repeat!

When they arrived, the door was unlocked so they walked on in to find their daughter sitting Indian style on the couch with the electrodes on her head just staring into their eyes, unable to speak! Adam was still carrying on and had to be settled down by the policeman. He grabbed Adam's arm and pushed him up against a wall, told him to cool it or be taken in! (Mrs. Watson knew, by what she had heard on the phone, that the yelling had started because of his jealousy of her being around so much during the day. But, Sara needed her and they worked together. She always made it a point to leave early and not interfere with their family time. He must have had a bad day at work to lose it like that.)

The policeman left when he knew she was okay and things were calmer. Adam was settled down and Sara was able to talk again. But she was upset and crying as she apologized for the drama and getting everybody out at such a late hour. Adam apologized and promised to stay calm the rest of the night. Then Sara went on to bed.

The next morning Mrs. Watson took Sara to see the neurologist that was monitoring the seizure activity to get the electrodes removed. It turned out that they recorded a pretty strong seizure the night before! The doctor said things at home had to stay calm. When she told Adam, he felt awful and was sincerely sorry.

That fall 911 was called a few times. Each time things were a little different that made them wonder if it was just a seizure. Adam seemed to be handling the stress a little better. Sara was put on seizure medicine, which helped; but she was still in need of God's healing powers!

## Chapter 17

# Holidays 2000

Adam and Sara treasured their fun with Jacob over Halloween trick-or-treating and family dinners on Thanksgiving. They made sure he got to see his cousins, Edward and Elizabeth, who lived in a nearby town. They both had their December birthdays. He turned one and she was five. Edward was in no rush to walk; he waited until his first birthday and made the day even more memorable. He was *running* through the house a few days later!

Since this was Adam and Sara's first Christmas, his grandparents bought their first Christmas tree for his December birthday present. He surprised her with it one day when he brought it in the front door. They were like two little kids picking out their first ornaments and lights. Jacob was in awe when the lights were turned on. Adam was doing a lot better and enjoying being a dad; the holidays made it so much fun.

The kids would all sit still through the story of Jesus that Christmas. The family took turns driving them around to look at Christmas lights and sang the traditional Christmas songs. Elizabeth was already good at learning lyrics; she was always singing along with the radio! She also liked entertaining the boys.

Sara was thankful for the disability checks she was receiving; it helped her feel she was contributing to the family budget even though she couldn't work. Though money was tight, they had a blast picking out things for Santa to bring Jacob! They knew that books had to be on that list because he loved to sit down with one after another. He would say, "More books". He was so little he would flip over and slide off the couch on his belly, waddle over to get another book, climb back on the couch and snuggle in to Sara's side, ready to go again!

They took Jacob to the Candlelight Service at church on Christmas Eve, and then went to open presents at Adam's parents' house. But seeing his face Christmas morning was worth a million bucks. Their hearts were filled with so much love for this little guy! After their Christmas morning, they took him to her parents' house to open presents. Having *little ones* around made Christmas fun again for everybody! Now the young adults appreciated their parents even more as they were getting a taste of the joys of parenthood.

New Year's Eve 2000 was coming up and they had to decide if they were going out or staying home. There had been no episodes with her head this month. But, she really didn't want to drink, dance, and stay out late at a party and chance stressing anything. It sounded good to cuddle up with her little family to bring in the year, so that's what they did. They watched over

Jacob sleeping at mid-night and then Adam swooped her up like he did on their honeymoon and took her to bed! They listened to fireworks going off in the neighborhood. She said, “Happy New Year!” Then he said, “Happy New Year, Baby; maybe this year won’t be so eventful and we can get on with our lives!” “Oh, I hope so!” she replied. What a ***year*** it had been!

# Chapter 18

# Adoption and More Gamma Knife?

As the New Year came in, there were things Sara wanted to get accomplished before her check up. She was afraid the doctor would say that the Gamma Knife had to be repeated. She knew she lost some memory last time and often words were hard for her to spit out. What else would she lose this time around? Being at high risk for disaster was hard enough to deal with. She sure wasn't up for any more surprises.

One of the things she wanted to accomplish was the adoption. Adam wanted to adopt Jacob, to give him his last name, and to *really* be his dad! They had saved up the $1000 attorney fee; so they called for an appointment with someone they knew. Adam was friends with the attorney's son. There was time for them the next day.

He was a little nervous going to the appointment, even though they were told it was a pretty simple process. Adam would have to appear in court before a judge and answer questions. He agreed, so the attorney would set it up and get back with them on the date and time.

When they got back to the truck, Sara asked, "If anything happens to me, do you promise with all your heart that you will take care of my son?" Adam said, "No . . . OUR son!" She kissed him and was quiet the rest of the way home. She prayed he was sincere.

Adam was still sort of easy to get frustrated. One day he started in again and then made a comment about having to take off work again to go in front of a judge. He said, "It's stupid bullshit to have to go to another appointment!" Sara blasted, "Listen Adam, it's a *privilege* to have my son as *your* son. If you're not 100% about this adoption, we'll drop it right now!" "No dammit, I'm not saying that; I'm just complaining about taking off work," he responded. "Well, complain to *yourself* then; I don't want to hear it! It sounds like it's too much trouble to make him yours," she said as a lump came in her throat and tears welled up in her eyes. "Sara, please stop this" he said. He walked over and cupped her face in his hands, "It's an emotional time for me too! I feel like he's already mine; I just hate the formalities. I love him and I love you so much; I can't imagine my life without either of you." "I'm sorry, it's just so important to me," she cried. "Me too, baby!" he replied as he hugged her and couldn't help but think about the baby they lost.

The call finally came with the time for court appearance. It was the next Thursday at 9:30. Sara's mom kept Jacob while they went to the appointment. They entered the courtroom just minutes before his case was called up. Adam stood before the judge, identified himself and took an oath to tell the truth. He was asked questions about parenting, paying for education and healthcare, and to protect Jacob from harm to the best of his ability. He promised all the above and was awarded Jacob as his son! Sara breathed a sigh of relief, "Thank you, God!" Adam's heart was pounding and tears welled up as he hurried to Sara. "He's *officially* mine!" They went to pick him up right away. He came running to the door when he saw it was them. Adam picked him up and raised him toward the ceiling, "Hey Buddy!" Then he brought him into a *family* hug, "I love you son." Grandma couldn't keep a dry eye with that scene and got in on the hug.

They took Jacob by Adam's mom's work to "introduce" her "grandson"! She picked him up and gave him big hug, "You all have to come by tonight for dinner; your dad will want to see him!" They promised they would and then Adam dropped them off at the apartment and went back to work for the rest of the day.

Meanwhile, Sara had made an appointment for her year exam with the neurosurgeon. He could see her the first week of February.

While Jacob was sleeping she put on her jacket and stepped out on their deck to breathe in the fresh January air and reflect on the past years. What a year...and she thought 1999 was rough! 2000 had topped it without a doubt! It was a miracle she was still here. She prayed, "Thank you, God for Jacob and Adam . . . and thank you for this year with them. It's been a wild ride."

February came quicker than she wished. Sara's mom kept Jacob while she and Adam went to the appointment in St. Louis. They went to Barnes Hospital for a CT scan then on to see the doctor. She was so nervous to get the results; she couldn't even carry on a conversation. When Sara couldn't *talk*...it was too *emotional*! She feared the pain of the screws in her head and the damaging affects of another intense radiation treatment.

The doctor came into the room with a puzzled look on his face, "Have you had lots of prayers going up?" "Yeah," she answered with a quivering voice, "Why?" "This thing is *gone*!" he said in disbelief. "What do you mean?" she asked and started to cry. "No more Gamma Knife?" as she about squeezed Adam's fingers off! "The AVM and aneurysm are *obliterated* . . . only a little scar tissue is left. I've *never* seen this happen within a year." He motioned for her to come up to the x-ray viewer, "I'll show you the difference from your first scan." He pointed to the AVM and aneurysm in the year-old images, then to the same areas in todays, "You have no more chance of a bleed than anyone else. Some things in medicine just *can't* be explained, that's where the *higher power* comes in. I think your neurologist at home can take it from here. If you have any questions or concerns with your left over side effects, please call me." Sara was already standing up doing little bounces with shaking hands over her mouth. "Oh, thank you *God* . . . and thank you doctor!" She reached to shake his hand and Adam did the same and said, "Thank you, sir!" As they were walking out the doctor said, "Enjoy your life young lady."

They both felt like they were walking on air! She picked up her phone and dialed her mom first. She said with a trembling voice, “Mom, call Dad on conference call . . . I want to talk to both of you at the same time.” “Okay,” she said nervously, then dialed her husband and told him Sara was on the phone. “Sara?” he said, like he was surprised she called him and instantly wondered what the news would be.

“Hey, Dad . . . It’s ***GONE***” she squealed! “What?” they both said at the same time! “It’s gone . . . like a *miracle*!" cried Sara, "No more Gamma Knife . . . and he said I'm no longer at high risk, no more chance of a bleed than anybody else!” “Oh dear God, it *is* a *miracle*!” cried her mom, “I’ll call your brother and *everybody* else!” Her dad sighed, “It’s gone.” That’s all he could say as he choked up; he had to hang up the phone. He put his head down toward his desk cupped with both hands, “It’s gone; you came thru Lord . . . it’s **gone**!” And he wept.

Two years later...

They were blessed to add a beautiful daughter to their family...“Eva” was their little princess!

*The End*

CPSIA information can be obtained at www.ICGtesting.com
Printed in the USA
LVOW12s2220130314

377375LV00001B/61/P